JUNGLE AMBUSH

The first burst of fire from my machine gun killed four of them. Mohammed Nabi got it first and he did a little dance before he fell down dead. The last two tried to make it to cover. One of them dived for the brush like a swimmer going into a pool. I killed him on the wing and he went head over heels before he hit the ground. One was left and he was in cover and returning my fire. But he was rattled and not making the best use of his weapon.

Bullets tore bark from the tree behind me. Another burst came, then stopped abruptly, and then I swung the light gun and raked his position with fire, running close to the end of the belt before I stopped firing. At first there wasn't a sound, then a strangled, sobbing noise came from the brush. I didn't move and I didn't fire. He might be crawling up on me, but I didn't think so. It was a bit late for tricks.

I picked up the knife and went down the slope to make sure he was dead. I found the last Moro in the brush, lying on his side, the AK-47 still in his hands.

Peter McCu...

LEISURE BOOKS ∞ NEW YORK CITY

A LEISURE BOOK

Published by

Dorchester Publishing Co., Inc.
6 East 39th Street
New York, NY 10016

Copyright©1984 by Dorchester Publishing Co., Inc.

Printed in the United States of America

ONE

To get into the Philippines all you need is a valid passport if you don't plan to stay more than twenty-one days. For longer visits, a passport with a visa issued by a Philippine consular official is required. After fifty-nine days a visitor must register with the Bureau of Immigration in Manila. A temporary visitor's visa is good for a year. I didn't expect to be there that long.

Americans ran the islands until 1946. Now they don't and you're not expected to forget it. The CIA may be the power behind the Marcos government, but ordinary Americans get no special privileges. Not unless they have plenty of money.

I had to come to Manila to see Mrs. Clifford D. Sanders. She lived in an old Spanish-style house about fifteen miles from the city. It had a neglected look, from the unwatered lawn to the cracked paint of the porch. It might have been a boarding house, but apparently she lived there alone with a Filipino housekeeper not much younger than herself. Not the kind of place you'd expect to find the widow of a famous American general.

She was a well preserved seventy or so, and it wasn't hard to picture her as the ambitious young wife of a brigadier general on MacArthur's staff. She had been a Southern blonde, gray now and still flighty in manner, but always with her eye on the main chance. Southern army posts used to have a lot of women like that, bossy and catty, all drawn from the same pool of officers' wives. In the old prewar army they had enlisted men doing their chores, even doing housework, now and then acting as studs when it was safe to do so. These latter-day Confederate belles flowered in the army posts of Dixie: snobbish, eager to get ahead, terrified of "Nigras." They lasted well into the 1950's, when things changed. They're still around, but not in such numbers. They're against equal rights for women because they've always been boss.

The housekeeper had olive skin, a hefty figure and slanted eyes; she spoke toneless, accentless English. She nodded when I said Mrs. Sanders was expecting me and led me down a dark hallway that opened into a darkened room. It was cool but airless in the house. There was the smell of furniture polish and elderly women. The room the housekeeper led me into looked like the set for a play set in the tropics. Leatherbound books went from floor to ceiling. There were faded photographs of American army officers and a few civilians. Nearly everybody in the pictures wore white. A few automobiles dated the photographs from the 1930's.

I had no idea of what Mrs. Sanders wanted, but she had sent an airline ticket and three hundred in cash. All I needed was one look at her to know that here was no hare-brained old lady but someone who knew what she was doing all the time. Back in the Thirties they used to call some super feminine movie star the Iron Butterfly. The description suited Mrs. Sanders down to the ground.

"You are most welcome, Mr. Rainey," she said in a soft Southern accent, waving a mottled, clawlike hand in a grand gesture. "I was just having a little sherry. Would you care to join me?"

"No thank you. I'm not much for sherry," I said.

She smiled, taking care not to crack the mask of her make-up. "I suppose not. What about a bottle of our fine Philippine beer?"

She rang a bell and the housekeeper brought a bottle of San Miguel and a glass.

"I know you have been in the military," Mrs. Sanders said. "But perhaps you are not familiar with General Sanders' career. After all, it was a long time ago and the world forgets so quickly."

I knew something about Sanders' career; he had a small but respectable place in American military history. He had been an aide to Mac-Arthur during his years of being commander-in-chief of the Philippine armed forces; had been with him on Corregidor and in Korea. He had resigned from the army after Truman fired Mac-Arthur for talking back. Sanders had risen to brigadier by then; in retirement, he wrote a book titled *Betrayal of the Philippines,* which

7

claimed that MacArthur was let down by the politicians back home.

"I know a little about General Sanders," I said, glad to be able to mention his book.

"I'm sure you haven't read it, Mr. Rainey. It's all ancient history now, but my husband was right, you know. The Washington politicians pushed for Philippine independence when they should have voted money to defend the islands. All the Japanese had to do was walk in. We had very few planes in the air."

I nodded. There was no point in disagreeing with an old lady. I sipped my beer and waited for her to go on.

"Colonel Kiley speaks very highly of you," she said. "That's how I got your name."

"Yes, you mentioned that in your letter."

She laughed. "I'm afraid I'm getting a little forgetful. Mr. Rainey, are you familiar with the island of Mindanao?"

"No, just Luzon. I've never been down south."

Mrs. Sanders treated herself to another tot of sherry and gave me a careful look. "I want you to go to Mindanao, to a small town called Evangelista, and buy back a diary that was kept by my husband. An American, John Ritter, has it in his possession, or he says he has. Ritter wants twenty thousand American dollars for the diary. I am prepared to meet his price. He has a villainous reputation, but I don't care about that."

An old ceiling fan creaked overhead. "What's in the diary?" I asked.

"Serious accusations against high ranking officers and politicians. Americans and Filipinos, but mostly Americans. Just before the

8

war, a number of large American companies were worried about losing their holdings in the islands. According to my husband's diary, these men bribed Washington politicians to oppose the independence movement. The liberals, mostly Democrats, were all for independence. I don't know if my husband really believed what he wrote in his diary. He's dead and what he believed hardly matters. The diary is a fake."

"Are you sure?"

"Quite sure. My husband never told me about it—he wrote it late at night in his study—but being a woman, and curious, I sneaked a look at it."

"Why does that make it a fake?"

"Because he used different pens, different inks, as if the diary had been written years before. But he completed the diary in less than a month."

"Yes, but what was his purpose?"

"The diary was to be made public after his death. I suppose he intended to give it to an attorney, but he died suddenly. His heart. Some of the men accused in the diary were MacArthur's enemies. Douglas had a way of rubbing important men the wrong way. When that little haberdasher Truman forced Douglas out of the army, my husband resigned, and we came back here to live. He could get quite violent about the way MacArthur was treated by the politicians. All his life he identified with Douglas. He regarded Douglas's ouster as a slap at himself."

I finished my beer and said, "Mrs. Sanders, it's hardly unusual for businessmen to bribe politicians. It doesn't go on as much as it used to, but they still do it. Besides, what these men are accused of happened more than forty years ago."

She gave me a sharp look. "I don't want to use the diary to do harm. Some of these men are still alive, and there were young lieutenants who are colonels or generals now. I don't want their careers ruined by my husband's malice."

"What else is in the diary?"

"Plans to seize the Philippines after the Japanese were defeated. No one expected them to win. It was only a matter of time before we beat them. The Philippines would get their independence and these businessmen would take over. My husband believed there was a conspiracy to steal an entire country. But there was no conspiracy. My husband didn't write his diary until 1956."

"All in one month?"

"Just as I described it to you. I want it back so it can be destroyed. I can't go to the police for obvious reasons. The Marcos government would like to get their hands on it. So would the Communist rebels. But Ritter has it and he's the one I have to deal with. Or rather, *you* have. Will you take the job?"

That was something to think about. There was a war going on in Mindanao. The Marcos government was fielding an enormous force in an effort to beat the Moro Communist rebels, who controlled a good part of the island. Moros had a well earned reputation for ferocity; they never took prisoners.

"I'll pay you twenty thousand dollars," Mrs. Sanders said, leaning forward in her high backed chair. "Twenty for Ritter and twenty for you. There is no use trying to bargain for more. It's all the money I have. Now will you take the job?"

"I'll take it. What do you know about Ritter?"

"Ritter is an American, born in Philadelphia. He's about forty and was a Marine guard at the embassy here. He killed a man in a bar fight and fled to Mindanao. The man he killed was another Marine, so the Filipinos aren't too interested. Besides, the government doesn't have much authority in that part of Mindanao. He is a desperate character by all accounts. He had a bad service record before he got into this final, serious trouble. A man like that should never have been an embassy guard. Mr. Rainey, the United States military is not what it used to be."

"Yes ma'am," I said.

"It gets worse every year. They shouldn't have done away with the draft. I was reading where many of the soldiers in this new all-volunteer, mostly-Negro army can barely read. They have to make up picture books for them so they can learn how to drive a tank. I ask you, how are we going to fight the Soviets with soldiers like that?"

I grunted. "How did Ritter get hold of the diary?"

Mrs. Sanders had a bit of sherry before she answered. "It was really by accident," she said. "We had a small sugar plantation near the village of Evangelista. That was in the Fifties, after the Korean War, Mr. Truman's police action, after my husband retired. It wasn't a going concern, just something to keep my husband

11

busy, keep him from brooding. Not that it did much good, I can tell you. My husband was a bitter man, Mr. Rainey. Be that as it may, after he died in 1956, I moved back here to Manila. Many of my friends urged me to go home, but where was 'home' after so many years in the islands? This was home, Manila was. I never liked Mindanao. Too hot and jungly. Too wild. Our house in Evangelista had been closed up for years. I tried to sell it, but was forced to keep it because no one would offer a decent price. The guerrilla war, naturally. As I say, this man Ritter happened on our house by accident. He fled to that part of the world because it was so remote, well beyond the reach of the law. He moved in and nobody tried to stop him. Nobody was there to stop him. I suppose the place looked abandoned. It *was* abandoned, in a way. One way or another, he found the diary where my husband had hidden it in a waterproof case."

"Did you know where it was hidden?"

"Of course not. If I had, I would have destroyed it after my husband's death. That should be obvious, Mr. Rainey."

"Yes ma'am. But you did look for it?"

There was a pause while she took a bracer. "I looked as well as I could. You know how it is when a loved one dies suddenly. Chaos, Mr. Rainey, utter chaos. You see, Clifford was in excellent health for a man of his age. Very fit. Then one day he simply collapsed and died. His heart, no warning. He must have known he was going to die. I suppose he did. He burned so many old files and records. I asked him why all this sudden activity and he laughed and said

12

there was too much junk lying around. He said, 'Let the dead past bury itself,' or words to that effect. That's a quotation from some poem, perhaps a play. I'm afraid I don't know which it is."

"Then you thought he might have burned the diary with the other stuff?"

"Yes, that was it," Mrs. Sanders said. "He used an old oil drum with holes punched in it. It was useful to burn papers he didn't want to put in the trash hole behind the house. I'm sure nothing he burned was classified material, but he was very security minded, so he burned it. There were many old files, Mr. Rainey. My husband had been a soldier for many years. In answer to your question, yes, it seemed a reasonable supposition that he burned the diary at the same time."

I looked at a photograph of General and Mrs. Sanders taken many years before. Only the high-crowned cap made the general appear slightly taller than his wife. He had a big head for such a small man; his jaw stuck out as if to warn other people not to get in his way. Like all small men, he looked conceited and cantankerous.

"But you weren't satisifed that he'd destroyed the diary? That was what made you search for it?"

"I told you I wasn't sure of anything," Mrs. Sanders said, a little irritated by the question. She smiled wearily, her way of telling me that she was old and tired and wanted to get this thing nailed down without so much palaver. "We were married for a lifetime, but my husband was a very private man. I respected his privacy. It was one of the things that made our marriage work. For example, this business with the diary. Perhaps another wife would have faced him with the fact that she knew all about it—how dangerous, futile and ill-considered it was. I wanted to confront him, to convince him that what he was doing was, well, quite mad. Not that he was mentally unbalanced, or anything like that. Anger, bitterness, were at the root of it. I wanted to confront him. Quite simply, I didn't dare. You're a young man, Mr. Rainey. It must be difficult for you to understand such an old-fashioned attitude."

"I can understand well enough, Mrs. Sanders."

That got me a smile and another beer. Mrs. Sanders rang for it and the housekeeper brought it in. I got a clean glass for the second beer. The housekeeper was solid rather than fat, moving around as if on casters. Her black eyes and expressionless face gave her a sinister air; she looked like one of those servants who insinuate themselves into positions of power. I figured she had been listening at the door.

"Perhaps you do understand," Mrs. Sanders said. "Simply let me say that if my husband's wish was not always my command, it was something to be respected. I hoped he'd destroyed the diary, but I couldn't be sure. I didn't stand over him while he burned his papers. I didn't watch from the window. He wouldn't have liked it. Then he died and there was no time to think about it. My husband was dead and the darned diary was of no importance. It wasn't until I was preparing to leave Evangelista for good that I even thought about it. Yes, I searched for it all through the house. I looked in all the places where he might have hidden it. A quick search but thorough enough. Naturally I didn't go to such extremes as prying up floor boards. I didn't find it, I gave up."

It sounded fairly reasonable, but there was something wrong with it. I couldn't decide what it was. "You don't think Ritter could have heard about the diary?" I said. "What I mean is, a deserter running away from the police stumbles into an empty house and finds something so well hidden that even you didn't find it. That's a lot of coincidence."

Mrs. Sanders filled her glass. "Coincidence is what it is, Mr. Rainey. It can't be anything else. You'll just have to accept it. There is no way Ritter could have learned of the diary's existence. How could he? I knew about it, no one else. What does it matter how he found it? Isn't it possible a man like that might have some notion that all old houses have money hidden in them? Gold coins from the Spanish period, some such foolishness?"

"Yes, it could be that," I admitted.

"The point is, Mr. Rainey, that this thug Ritter has the diary and is threatening to sell it if I don't give him the money. Now you're going to ask me, why doesn't he just sell the diary and have done with it? It would seem that at least one of the men named in the diary would be glad to buy it. I'm afraid I have no ready answer for you. Perhaps Ritter is afraid to be so bold as to try that kind of blackmail. I just don't know. He is safe enough where he is as long as he doesn't become too notorious. Perhaps he thinks it's safer to deal with me, a helpless old

15

woman. Twenty thousand may be a great deal of money, to him . . ."

Mrs. Sanders' voice trailed off as if the effort to explain had been too much for her. The housekeeper came in to remind her that it was time to take her medication. Her black eyes damned me for asking too many questions; no doubt about it, she had been listening at the door.

"Don't fuss, Zoya," she fretted. "It's terrible to get old," she said to me. She used a sip of sherry to get the pill down and dabbed at her lips with a lace handkerchief, waiting for the housekeeper to go. I drank some beer.

The housekeeper closed the door and Mrs. Sanders took a slug of sherry. Her greedy way of drinking the sherry was unpleasant to watch. It wasn't even the longing alcoholics have for liquor. Mrs. Sanders would be greedy for everything; there was a greedy child hidden in that withered body.

"This may be important," I said. "Have you told anyone else about the diary?"

"No one, Mr. Rainey."

"You're sure?"

"Of course I'm sure," the old woman said impatiently. "I didn't even tell Colonel Kiley because he said he didn't want to know. Something about your way of doing things."

I suppressed a smile. That sounded like Bob Kiley. I'd known him since we worked for the Phoenix Group, the special assassination section, in the early days of Vietnam War. I wasn't sure what he did now; it was sure to be clandestine. A very hard guy who sometimes threw work my way.

" 'Loose lips sink ships,' " Mrs. Sanders said, quoting the old World War Two anti-espionage slogan. She smiled. "I know what good security means, Mr. Rainey. I wasn't married to a career soldier for nothing. Now the question is, will you take the job?"

I nodded. "I'll take it."

"I'd like you to go to see Ritter as soon as possible. I'm afraid something will happen to him and the diary will fall into the wrong hands. It will be a relief when it's safely destroyed."

"Wouldn't it be better if I destroyed it?" I said. "Mindanao is a long way from here. Dangerous country. Things happen."

Again there was that sharp look. "No, I want it back so I can destroy it myself. Burn it and rake the ashes. It's not that I don't trust you, you understand."

"That's all right. You're the one paying to get it back. I'm going to need a gun just in case Ritter tries any funny business. By any chance did General Sanders have pistols in the house? It's not easy for a stranger to get a gun in Manila and I don't want any trouble with the police. An army issue forty-five would do just fine."

Mrs. Sanders got up and went to a desk by the window. She unlocked it and took out a wool-lined leather holster with the flap tightly buckled. The forty-five she handed me glistened with gun oil; there was cleaning gear and a box of shells to go with it.

"As you see, Clifford's service pistol is in perfect condition," she said. "The ammunition is new, but you'll want to check it yourself. My husband taught me the care and handling of

17

guns. I have another forty-five just like it upstairs in my bedside table. These lovely islands have become so dangerous in recent years."

She watched me while I checked out the semi-auto and the ammunition. When your life depends on a gun, you can't take anybody's word that it will fire. But there was no need to check this one. It had been well looked after. I wiped it clean with a soft cloth and put it where it wouldn't make a bulge.

"Now for Ritter's money and your fee," Mrs. Sanders said, unlocking another drawer. "Please count it, Mr. Rainey. We might as well be businesslike. You'll find it comes to exactly forty thousand dollars."

The count came out right and I asked her if she wanted a receipt. "There's no need," she said, shaking her head. "I have Colonel Kiley's guarantee that you're a most dependable man." The money was in my pocket, but she pointed anyway. "I don't mind telling you that's practically all the money I have in the world. But what does it matter at my age? I live modestly and my wants are few. Mostly what I want is to get this diary problem settled. It shouldn't have happened, but it did. Life is strange, isn't it?"

I said it was.

Mrs. Sanders put her bony hand on my arm and smiled up at me; it didn't take much imagination to see her doing the Southern belle bit forty years before. A tough old catfish.

"You won't let me down, will you, Mr. Rainey?"

"I'll do my best," I said, manly as all get-out. There was something fishy about her, but then I have a suspicious nature; it didn't have to mean anything. General Sanders may have worn the pants in the family—why shouldn't he? He was a man and was expected to wear pants—but his wife had been the real mover and shaker; there was some mystery here, as there is in all families.

"It was difficult when Clifford was alive," she went on. "I depended on him so. Now I must depend on you. I like you, Mr. Rainey, and even without Colonel Kiley's recommendation I think I'd be ready to trust you. The colonel tells me you're from Texas."

"Beaumont," I said.

"Lovely place," Mrs. Sanders said. "You may have guessed I'm a Southerner myself. Macon, Georgia, originally. I always say there's nothing like people from your own part of the country. I feel as if I've known you for years."

I was glad when she let go my arm; it was like being clawed by a ghost. A floorboard creaked in the hall and I knew the half-ton housekeeper was still out there, listening. I wished there was some quick way I could get some background on Sanders and his widow, but there wasn't time. I had no contacts in Manila; to start asking questions could bring the police down on me. All I could do was go with what I had.

"Mr. Rainey," the old woman said, sitting down again, "why don't you have another beer and I'll tell you how to get to Evangelista."

TWO

I flew to Zamboanga City from Manilla. The 450 mile trip took about two and a half hours. Coming in to land, I saw Moslem fishing villages built on stilts over the sea. I expected it to be as hot as hell, but it wasn't. The war didn't seem to have affected it; the streets were jammed with tourists. Mrs. Sanders' forty-five was in my checked-through luggage: one suitcase with shirts, shorts, shaving gear. There were soldiers and police all over the place, but to them I was just another tourist.

I rented a car from an American who ran an agency near an old Spanish fort. This guy had a crew cut and the look of an ex-GI and he stared hard when I said I wanted to get to Evangelista. "You'll have to leave a cash deposit," he said. "You may run into the Moros."

I gave him the money and he said Evangelista was about ninety miles away, in the interior of the island. "You won't like it there, buddy. The Moros have been killing and burning everything in sight. But it's your funeral, right?"

It got hotter as I drove inland and the town gave way to green marshy fields. After that the rain forest took over. Along the road were houses, a few shrines devoted to the Virgin. At one point a Philippine Scouts patrol had a road-block up, but they passed me through without giving me a hard time. The air conditioner wasn't working and I sweated hard in the merci-less heat. I came to a tiny village and drank two beers.

Two hours later I was coming into Evangel-ista. There were no soldiers in sight; the village looked dead. On all sides of it the rain forest came in close, seeming to shut off the air. This was the real southeast Asia, so very different from Manila that it might have been another country. The few people I saw looked like Mus-lims, and their faces were far from friendly. These people had never been completely subdued, not by the Spanish, not by the Ameri-cans. I hoped I wouldn't be taken for a govern-ment agent and shot in the back.

I went into the only bar in town and got a beer from a fierce-faced Moro with his head bound up in bright cloth. All he did was grunt when I asked him where I could find the American, Rit-ter. English didn't get me anything, so I tried Spanish. Still no luck. I was leaving the bar when a tiny Filipino greeted me in English. He wore a loud print shirt and a porkpie hat and he grinned at the sweat stains under my arms.

"Hot enough for you?" he said. "You look wasted, man."

"I am wasted. You know where I can find an American named John Ritter? Used to be a Marine. They tell me he looks like one."

"He looks like one. I hope he isn't a friend of yours. People here think he's a bad bastard. So do I."

I looked at this tiny wise-guy. "You're not from here, are you?"

He had eyes like black olives. "Shit no, man. I'm from Manila. Before that, L.A. I got into a jam with the biggest hood in Manila and he put out a contract on me. I'm safe enough as long as I stay out here in the boondocks. Hey, how about buying me a beer? I'm all tapped out and there's no way to make any money down this way. The Moros leave me alone and I keep out of their way."

We went back into the bar and I got him a beer. I nursed my own beer. I was sweating like a bull. "What about Ritter?" I asked.

"He's got a beat-up house not far from town. A real dump. He's got a couple of broads, not Moros, living with him. Drinks most of the time, doesn't do it in town. Buys his shit and takes it home. I don't know what he did in Manila. It must have been pretty bad to land him here. Me, I'm just a smalltime dope dealer that got on the bad side of the wrong gang. What's your name, by the way?"

I told him.

"Mine is Federico Aduana. Call me Freddy. Maybe you need an interpreter?"

"I don't need an interpreter to talk to Ritter."

"You never know what you're going to need if you stay here."

"No chance of that. You want to show me the way to Ritter's? There's a few bucks in it for you. Have another beer and we'll go out there."

He might be a government agent, but I didn't

think so. I was carrying a lot of money and couldn't be sure he wasn't working with some local bad lads. Even so, I was ready to take a chance on him. And I'd shoot him if I had to.

We drove out of town and the road grew narrower and in places the trees formed an arch, dark and green and damp. "Is there any place I can stay if Ritter isn't around?" I asked.

Freddy was fiddling with the radio, trying to get something besides static. "Ritter never goes anywhere, which makes me think he's hiding from the cops. If by some chance he's away, then you can stay with me. There's no hotel in Evangelista and you can't sleep in the car."

"We'll see," I said. "How can you stand it here?"

"Where would I go? I've got no money. You want to stake me to plane fare to L.A.?"

"Can't do it."

"Turn in here," Freddy said, "and watch your springs. This road is all shot to hell."

I drove down a narrow road that had been surfaced years before. Now it was potholed and grown over with weeds. There was a break in the trees and I saw a big frame house that was busy falling down. It looked at least forty years old, maybe older than that.

"Who used to live here?" I asked.

"People named Sanders or Saunders," Freddy answered. "Old man was a retired general and a big crazy, I hear. He died and his old lady moved away, maybe back to the states. Way back there was land cleared for sugar. Nothing came of it, a bust."

We were close to the house when there was a

24

burst of gunfire. It sounded like an M-2 and the person using it was shooting off a whole clip. None of the bullets came our way, but Freddy ducked down in alarm. "Shit man, we better get out of here. That could be Moros."

"Calm down," I said. "You stay in the car or walk back to town. I may be a while."

"Doing what?"

"Talking to Ritter. What are you going to do?"

"Hide behind the car," Freddy said.

I stuck the forty-five in my waistband and went down the road, taking it slow. It was quiet except for some bird making a racket. Then there was the sound of a clip being slapped into place. Immediately after that came another burst of gunfire and the shattering of whisky bottles. The firing went on until the clip was empty.

"Ritter!" I yelled. "Ritter! Knock it off, I'm coming in. I'm not a cop. Mrs. Sanders sent me."

There was a pause while he made up his mind what to do. Then he yelled back, "Come forward with your hands on your head."

The house was set back from the road. Ritter had taken cover just inside the door and the barrel of the M-2 moved to cover me as I got close. There were broken bottles and food cans strewn all over what had once been a front yard. The food cans stank as flies buzzed in and out of them. An old Chevrolet was parked by the side of the house, out of the sun.

Ritter came out on the porch with the carbine aimed at my chest. He was drunk, bleary-eyed, swaying on his feet. "Keep your hands on top of your head," he warned. "I can shoot you five times before you make a move. You bring the money, asshole?"

"I brought it. Where's the diary?"

"Never mind that. How much money did you bring?"

"Twenty thousand. That's what you asked for."

Ritter was a brute of a man with clipped blond hair, tiny blue eyes, a big chin. He must have been a typical Marine before the booze got to him. I could smell h is sweat at ten feet.

"Twenty thousand isn't enough," he said. "I changed my mind. Leave the twenty here, then go back and get thirty more. Fifty thousand is about right."

"The money's in the car. I'll go get it."

"You do that if you want the diary." Ritter staggered and nearly fell, but he brought up the M-2 before I could get close to him. "Go get the money and then we'll talk about the rest of the money. If the old biddy wants the diary, she'll have to pay."

I went back to the car and Freddy said, "You can't deal with a maniac like that. I don't know what your business is with him, but you'll get killed for sure."

"You're right. I'll come back in the morning. Maybe he'll be halfway sober by then." It was starting to get dark. "Where do you live? You got any food in the house?"

Freddy grinned. "Not a lot. I eat when I can, not that often. You feel like steak?"

"Yeah, steak and cold beer wouldn't be bad."

"The beer won't stay cold for long. One more time I'm telling you, watch out for that Ritter.

Out here he can kill you and get away with it."

We got steak and beer and drove out to Freddy's shack at the end of town. It was just two rooms with a packed dirt floor, but it was clean. Freddy put the steak in a pan on the kerosene stove and we drank beer while it cooked. On the wall there was a photograph of downtown L.A. clipped from some magazine. Freddy saw me looking at it. "I should never have left there," he said, dreamy-eyed.

"Why did you?"

"I had a difficulty with the cops. I should have done my time instead of jumping bail. I'd be there now. Ah shit, I'm a real fuck-up, you know that."

"Don't let the steak burn," I said.

"You come a long way to talk to Ritter. You want to tell me what about?"

"No, I don't, Freddy."

Freddy got up and lit a kerosene lamp. "The village has electricity. Mine's cut off. Kerosene stinks, but you can see by it. All that free beer made me sleepy, man. I'm going to bed."

Freddy slept in one room, I slept in the other. It got cooler after it got dark. A truck passed on the road. Freddy muttered in his sleep. I was too tired to care. I'd come all the way from San Francisco, then from Manila to Zamboanga in little more than a day, and I was beat. During the night I thought I heard gunfire, but I couldn't be sure, because it was so far away.

Freddy was up before I was. He made strong black coffee and handed me a cup. "You hear the shooting last night?" he asked.

"Yeah, I heard it. What do you think it was?"

"I don't know what it was, but it came from

out by Ritter's place. I think maybe you shouldn't go there today."

I finished my coffee and headed for the car. "I have to go," I said. "I'm getting paid for this."

I left the car halfway to the house and went ahead on foot. Ritter's body lay sprawled on the porch steps with two Filipino girls crying over him. They jumped up in fright when they heard me coming. "Wait," I shouted, but that only frightened them more. They ran and disappeared.

Ritter had been riddled with bullets. His chest was all chewed up and the back of his head was gone. Whoever shot him wanted to make sure he was dead. Blue flies were buzzing around his wounds; ants ran in and out of his open mouth.

The inside of the house was filthy, but I had to search for the diary. I dug around in corners and closets, looked under mattresses until there was nowhere else to search. Then I found the keys to the old Chevrolet and looked in the trunk and under the seats. No diary.

I left the body where it was and drove back to Freddy's shack. "All that shooting was Ritter," I said. "He got it good."

"But why would anyone want to kill him? He was an animal, but he bothered no one in the village. Why don't you tell me about it?"

So I told him.

"What a crazy story," he said, shaking his head. "Even TV shows aren't that crazy."

"They used automatic weapons," I said. "You think they're Moros?"

Freddy looked scared. "Yes, that's what I think. Rainey, my friend, you bought me steak

28

and beer and cigarettes. Why don't you go back to the States and forget this old woman and her diary? If you want to be honorable, why don't you give her back her money?"

"That would be bad for my business, Freddy. An old friend recommended me for the job and I can't screw it up. I have to see it through."

"Then what do you want to do?"

"I think the Moros have the diary. I have to find them and pay for it if I have to. What language do they speak?"

"Most of them speak Filipino, others speak some English or Spanish. You can make yourself understood if they let you live long enough. But they won't. They'll take the money and torture you to death. They hate Americans as much as they hate Filipinos. Don't forget they're Communists."

I opened a warm beer and gave it to Freddy, then got one for myself. "Do you know where the Moros are?"

"Yes. They're east of here, far back in the hills. They've been keeping quiet lately. You can't go in there, Rainey. I think they're the worst guys alive. You must have read about their war with the Americans. They tied their balls with leather thongs so the pain would be so bad they'd feel no fear. They tied their balls and ran against machine guns. Every Filipino knows that story."

"So do I. I still have to go. I'll pay you very well if you guide me in. You don't have to come all the way. Once we get close enough you can turn back."

Freddy lit a cigarette and got ashes all over his shirt. "See how nervous I am—no, I'm not just nervous. I have the piss scared out of me. You're a madman."

"Don't you want to go back to Los Angeles? Take me to the Moros and I'll give you the plane fare, plus some extra money. You're rotting here and you hardly know it. Go back to L.A. in style, wearing good clothes and smoking a cigar. What do you say?"

Freddy look a slug of beer. "It will take whisky to get me up into that country."

"You'll get whisky. Just don't fall down on me. A week from now you'll be in L.A. getting laid after eating a lobster dinner."

"If I'm not dead," Freddy said.

I had taken Ritter's carbine and five extra clips. The carbine was designed for use by officers during World War II and it was still regulation issue in Korea. It's a semi-auto, a good enough weapon in its way, but you don't see it much anymore, and though I've used it occasionally, it's not my favorite weapon. Now I checked it out and Freddy looked at it with a dismayed expression.

"I'd like it if you had a better gun," he said. "The Moros have AK-47's and M-16's. It will be like hunting tigers with an air gun."

"We'll get something better as we go along. Here, you take the forty-five. You know how to use it?"

"What's there to know, Rainey? You snap the slide and shoot until it's empty. Then you load another clip and keep on shooting. I don't think the Moros will be too scared of it."

"They'll be scared if you hit them," I said. "Now let's go and get the whisky and some supplies. What's the country like back there?"

"Scrubby hills and ravines, good places to hide. The last soldiers to go in there were slaughtered. The Moros have been ambushing soldiers for years. They know how to do it."

"Stop bellyaching and let's go," I said.

We drove down the street to the bar and the fierce-faced Muslim who ran it came up with everything we wanted. Not a word was said during the entire transaction. He wrote the amount due on a slip of paper and handed it to me.

"I think he's a spy for the Moros," Freddy said as we drove away. "By tonight they'll know there's a strange American in the hill country. They'll be looking for us. You think you can pay me my money now?"

"You think I'm going to get killed?"

"Well, a guy can't be too careful."

I grinned at the shifty little bastard. He was a drug pusher, but I liked him well enough. In my business you take people as you find them, which wasn't to say that he might not run out on me.

"How much do you want?" I asked him.

"Is a thousand dollars too much?"

"Not if you come through for me. I'll give you five hundred now, five hundred when we find the Moros."

I gave him the money and he grinned happily. "Maybe I didn't ask for enough, Rainey. You're a rich American and I am just a poor Filipino."

"Dry up," I said.

People watched us as we drove out of town. We headed east on the rutted road. Freddy had a few nips from the bottle and passed it to me. I

31

took one slug and gave it back to him.

"Don't drink it all," I said. "I want you to be able to see straight when we get up in the hills. Who leads the Moros in this district?"

"Mohammed Nabi is his name and they say he's been to China. A lot of Moros have been there. After they're trained, they come back to Mindanao. Mohammed Nabi wants to get up an independent Communist state in Mindanao. The Red Chinese supply him with weapons and they provide training for his men. It's a brutal war, but the Moros are sure they can win. Marcos is just as sure they want to take over the whole country and not just Mindanao. I think so too. I don't give a shit. I'm going back to L.A., and Marcos and the Moros can go to hell."

"Hey, I told you to go easy on the booze."

Freddy hiccuped and grinned. "Don't worry, my friend, I am going to be very brave with the general's forty-five. I was scared when we started out, but now I'm like a tiger."

We were coming out of the jungle. Up ahead were lines of rolling hills dotted with scrub and brownish rocks. A hot wind blew hard. It was better than the stinking heat of the jungle. The engine was overheating and I stopped to let it cool off.

We got out of the car and I said, "Where are we now?"

"Very close," Freddy answered. "We'll have to leave the car and walk in. You still think you can deal with the Moros?"

"I don't know. You feel like going back? If we're that close, I won't need you anymore."

Freddy didn't like that. "That's a lousy thing

to say to a friend. I'll go with you to protect the other half of my money."

I scouted the countryside with a pair of binoculars. All I saw was scrub and waving sun-browned grass. A small brown animal ran across the road and disappeared in the brush. Birds flew away in a flutter of wings. That was the only sign of life.

"Where does this road go?" I asked.

"Nowhere. The Moros blew it up in four or five places. Even a jeep would have trouble getting through. Your car will be burned not long after we leave it. What they can't use they destroy. You should know that."

"Okay, so now I know it. You coming or going?"

"God help me, I'm coming." Freddy took the forty-five from his pocket and snapped the slide. Then he put it back.

"Put the safety on," I warned him. "You may shoot your balls off if you don't."

"I'd hate to do that, now the good life is in sight. You think there's a chance I'll get to do that? You won't screw me, will you, pal?"

"You sound like an old woman I know. Put the God damned safety on!"

Freddy made the gun safe. "What old woman?"

"Forget it. You won't be screwed."

We started up into the hills. Their bright green color made them seem slightly unreal. They were the greenest hills I'd seen since Vietnam. This was country just made for guerrillas; no wonder the government counterinsurgency forces hadn't been making much headway. Miles ahead of where we were, the hills rose up to become jagged peaks. A small army could go in there and never be heard of again. It was hot and the air shimmered.

Freddy was right about how dangerous it was. What begins as a fairly simple trade, money for a diary, had turned into something infinitely more complicated. The Moros were at least as ferocious as the Viet Cong, and that was saying something. They might trade, they might not; all I could do was go in there and see what happened. Returning Mrs. Sanders' money never occurred to me. In my business you're only as successful as your last job. Word gets around. Back out of too many jobs and the jobs stop coming.

Freddy knew the country, but he wasn't in shape for it. He said he'd been a dope dealer. I guessed he'd been as much pimp as drug peddler. Men who work that side of the street can be tough enough. Just the same, it isn't the right training for fast travel in hard country. An hour after we left the road, Freddy was ready to fall down.

"You sure you know where we're going?" I said, thinking I could needle him out of his exhaustion. His clothes were sweated clear through and he was gasping for breath.

"What do you think? Course I know where we're going. Out of shape is all that's wrong with me. Let me rest a while and I'll be okay."

We sat on a dead tree and I gave him a drink of water. "I shouldn't of drank all that booze," he said, fanning himself with his stained panama hat. "But I wouldn't of come if I hadn't drank the booze. It gives you nerve, but it makes you tired. This is pretty important to you, huh?

34

Never mind, you don't want to tell me what's going on."

"Don't talk so much, you won't be so tired," I said.

I had Ritter's carbine ready to shoot if it came to that. It might. Where we were was all scrubby hills and rocks; a dark line in the distance was where the rain forest began. The sky was a harsh, bright blue with no clouds in it. I sipped water while Freddy lit a cigarette with shaky fingers.

I had a thought. "When was your last business with the Moros, Freddy? Don't tell me you haven't done a little work there."

Freddy shrugged. "Yeah, a little business now and then. I admit to that. One hand washes the other. I mean, when there's something they can't get with a gun. A few things they can't get with a gun. They can force themselves to stop killing when they have to. That goes against their nature, you dig? I didn't say I was friends with them. You're not another Moro, you can't be a friend."

"What did they buy? Information?"

"Sure, why not? I'm in the village. I make a few trips to Zamboanga, or I used to, before my car died. Now there's not so much information. What I did sell wasn't that important."

There were ants in the log. I stood up and brushed them off my pants. In the tropics something is always trying to eat you. I looked at Freddy, still sucking on his cigarette. Freddy was a miser with his smokes; he smoked them right down to his nicotine-stained fingers.

"You're saying your information wasn't reliable?"

"I'm saying no such thing. I'm saying it was no big thing. In Zamboanga, when I manage to get there, I listen to what I hear in the bars. Maybe I see a lot of new soldiers, some special unit that wasn't there my last visit. What I see, I report. The Moros have to decide what it's worth, then pay me. They don't pay much, they don't like to pay at all."

"And maybe you sell a little information to the soldiers?"

"Hey, that's too risky. Okay, maybe a little that doesn't mean much. I don't like Moros, but he pays better. You want the truth? I'm pissing my pants when I have to deal with either side. Bad people, both of them. But a guy has to live, am I right?"

"I wouldn't want the Moros to be too mad at you," I said.

Freddy waved my doubts away; they didn't go far. But what the hell! The little guy was a fixer, a go-between; wars couldn't be fought without guys like Freddy. I hoped the Moros subscribed to this idea.

"Naw, they ain't mad at me," Freddy said. "It's like we do a little business, not too much, and a guy can't be right a hundred percent of the time. It's like when you're panning for gold, right? You shovel in some gravel and hope you'll strike it rich."

Freddy shoveled shit instead of gravel; the little bastard had seen too many westerns; you can't pan for gold in a sewer. In a bar he might have been amusing for about five minutes. Out here I couldn't manage more than a sour smile.

"Let's go," I told him. "We could be taking a walk in the park for all the good it's doing."

Freddy climbed to his feet and slapped at the ants. They were all over him, but he'd been too tired to get up. He looked like a busted bookie on the run from his creditors.

"Some park," he said. "Some walk. You should of nailed that crazy Marine before the Moros got to him. You're such a tough guy, you oughtn't of let him scare you off like that. Now you got to walk all over these fucking mountains looking for what you should of got in the first place."

"Don't get nasty." I made sure the cap on the canteen was tight. The little weasel was right: it had been a mistake to waste time with Ritter. While I was waiting for him to sober up, the Moros had been coming down from the mountains.

We were climbing another long hill. "Speaking of parks," Freddy said. "You ever been in Griffith Park in L.A.?"

I was watching the line of trees; the rain forest was getting closer. "What about it?" I said, going along with his bullshit. He was less nervous when he talked.

"I used to pick up broads there," Freddy said. "I had my own technique worked out. Other guys go after knockouts and maybe score three percent of the time. I zeroed in on the dogs and was batting a thousand. I mean, all I wanted was to get laid, not a lifetime romance . . ."

He went on like that.

THREE

Suddenly, an hour later, there were Moros all around us. They just rose up out of the brush on both sides of the brushy ravine. I had been waiting for them to do that; now here they were. All were warmed with AK-47's, the favorite weapon of guerrillas everywhere, and they made hardly a sound. Good fighters, the best. A dark-faced man in his early thirties gestured with his rifle and I told Freddy to put his hands up. He didn't have to be told. I threw the carbine in the sand and a young Moro snatched it up. Another slapped Freddy around and took the forty-five.

The dark-faced man was the leader; he talked plain, functional English. "Who are you and what do you want? Did you think you were safe because you come with this pimping Filipino for a guide? Now the pimp carries a gun."

I knew without being told that this was Mohammed Nabi. He had the stern, humorless face of the fanatic, the absolute conviction that his cause was just beyond all question.

Freddy must have been braver or hungrier for money than I thought, to have dealings with this man.

I said, "I'm an American and my name is Rainey. Are you Mohammed Nabi?"

He ignored the question. "Tell me what you are doing here or I will shoot you here and now."

Well, that was direct enough. "I'm here to buy back General Sander's diary. You killed Ritter and took it. I can offer you twenty thousand for it. I have the money in my pocket."

Mohammed Nabi's dark, handsome face twisted itself into a smile of contempt. "Throw it on the ground, Yankee. Your money is no good here. You must be insane to come into these hills."

I tossed the money at his feet and waited to see what he was going to do. He motioned to one of his men; the money was picked up and given to Mohammed Nabi, who counted it with no show of interest.

"The diary is a fake," I said. "I suppose you've read it."

"With some amusement, Yankee. I don't care what it is. It will be used to show up the Yankees for what they are. They are fascist thugs and murderers. Were you paid to come here?"

"I was paid by Mrs. Sanders. She told me the diary is a fake and I believe her. Most of the men named in it have been dead for many years. There was no conspiracy. General Sanders was a crazy old man looking for revenge."

"The diary will be believed when it is shown to the world. It is in Sanders' handwriting. That can be established without difficulty. But that does not concern me at the moment. What do you think I should do with you? You are an American agent, a spy. You and this pimping Filipino are spies."

I was about to answer him when he raised his AK-47 and cut down Freddy with a hail of bullets. The little man was dead before he hit the ground. He hadn't been much of a man, but he'd been some kind of friend.

"You lousy son of a bitch," I said. "You didn't have to do that."

The AK-47 came up and I expected to die on my feet. All he did was spit on the ground in front of me. "The dirty little Filipino was nothing, but the Americans may pay something for you. How much are you worth, Yankee?"

Freddy lay dead not five feet away from me, the poor little crook. Whatever he was, he was better than this fanatic with his moral certainties.

"I'm worth nothing to the American government," I said. "I'm not with the CIA or any other agency. I have no interest in politics."

"Then you are a mercenary?"

"That's what I am. Your rotten little war is no concern of mine."

He showed anger for the first time. "So you think we are little brown men fighting for a hopeless cause. We beat you in Vietnam and we'll beat you here. We'll beat you everywhere, Yankee. You and your corrupt democracy are a thing of the past. I should kill you, but I'm going to hold you for a while. Maybe you are not an American agent. You could be lying. Time will tell what you are."

Mohammed Nabi snapped his fingers at one of his men. "Tie his hands behind his back. Tie them tight."

They tied my hands, then put a rope around my neck and dragged me away from there. No one looked at Freddy; to them he was just a carcass, a hunk of dead meat.

There was an explosion in the distance and I knew they had blown up my car. It didn't make any difference; a wrecked rental car was the last thing I had to worry about. The man leading me at the end of the rope was having a good time, yanking on the rope so that I fell on sharp rocks. By the time we got out of the long ravine, my clothes were ripped to shreds and I was bleeding from a dozen small wounds. Now and then, to get in the spirit of the thing, one of the Moros would come up close and spit in my face or kick me from behind. When that happened, they would laugh in the mindless way some Orientals have. The ravine climbed up to a long, low plateau, and when we crossed it, there was another ravine deeper and longer than the first one. Once I fell and hit my head and blacked out and came to only when one of the Moros burned my fingers with a cigarette lighter. Jesus, how I longed to get behind an AK-47 and cut them down.

We traveled on for miles and the hot wind blew fine sand in my face, clogging my nose, stinging my eyes. There were about twenty Moros in this party, but I knew they weren't fighting a guerrilla war with that few men. Mohammed Nabi fell back from the head of the column and walked beside me, talking in a conversational tone as if we were out for a stroll.

42

"You know the diary is not a fake," he said, smoking a brown paper cigarette with greedy puffs. "You know it isn't a fake, so you might as well admit it." He had a way of repeating himself, as if he could get to me by saying it often enough. "It can't be a fake or Mrs. Sanders would not have sent you. She would have been willing to pay twenty thousand dollars for something fraudulent."

"It has no value," I said, trying to stay on my feet.

"I think you are stupid enough to believe that," he said, lighting a fresh cigarette from the butt of the other. His fingers were brown with nicotine stains. He smoked all the time and I hoped lung cancer was creeping up on him. "You are wondering how I knew Ritter had the diary?"

I was in pain and I told him to go fuck himself. That got me a slap in the face, then he went on talking as if nothing had happened. He was a vain man and wanted to impress me.

"Ritter boasted about having it. A French journalist came to Evangelista and Ritter told him about it. He was drunk and thought the Frenchman's newspaper would pay a lot of money for it. The Frenchman didn't believe him, so he got nothing. Word of the diary finally got to me."

"How about untying my hands?" I said. "I'll be crippled if you don't take them off."

He patted his pockets, looking for another crumpled cigarette. "I don't mind if you are crippled," he said mildly, and there was no doubt that he meant what he said. "You Yankees must get out of Asia and stay out. You

43

have no place here, you never had any place here. See, you are hardly able to stand up. You should have stayed in the land of Coca Cola."

Mentioning Coke sent him into a rage and he threatened to blind me, to cut off my balls and stuff them down my throat. But, after he got through yelling like a maniac, all he did was talk some more.

"The general's diary will be sent to China, then the whole world will know about it. It will be translated into many languages."

"You said all that before."

He slapped my face, bringing blood from my mouth. If ever a man needed killing, this guy did. "You will hear it until you are sick of it. Pull him down and drag him," he ordered the Moro holding the rope.

I tried to fight the pull, but it was no use. My feet went out from under me and I twisted so I'd fall on my shoulder instead of my face. All the Moros turned to laugh. They let me up after dragging me for a hundred yards. By then we had come several miles from the first ravine and Mohammed Nabi told the Moros to rest and eat. I got a few swallows of water and a piece of bread; the Moro pulling the rope held the canteen and the bread up to my mouth and smiled as if we were the best of friends.

Mohammed Nabi sat nearby and went on with his political harangue. "See, Yankee, you are helpless. That young man pulling the rope cannot read or write, but he holds the power of life and death over you. There is nothing you can do about it. In a few years, after he has been educated, he will become an officer in our new national army. Can your country say the same of its illiterates, its blacks and Hispanics? Not all these men are destined for great things—some will die—but many will take their places in our new government. Marcos will be tried and hanged as a war criminal. Your CIA will not be able to prevent it."

I raised my head to look at him. "What will you be? What do you think you'll be? Revolutions have a way of killing off the original revolutionaries. Someday you may be dragged at the end of a rope."

He was surprised, or pretended to be. "Are you angry because you have been treated this way? How should we treat you if not as a criminal? Can such treatment possibly be a cruel and inhuman as what you Americans did in Vietnam? When I think of Vietnam, I think of Lieutenant Calley and what he did at My Lai. I think of napalm and Agent Orange. I think of the bombings of hospitals in Hanoi. And you think you have been badly treated!"

The Moros were listening, though I don't think any of them understood English. But they knew he was lecturing me and they nodded their approval. Some were very young, hardly more than boys, but they carried Chinese copies of Soviet automatic rifles, and that made them men.

"If you're going to kill me, why don't you do it?" I was weary of the fanatic and his endless talk. "You don't have to lecture me to death. I told you I don't give a damn about your politics. Your politics or anyone else's."

Mohammed Nabi gave me a thin smile. "You have the courage of a very stupid. Do not rush to embrace death, Yankee. We are Communists

45

but also we are Moros. Muslims. If we kill you, you will scream for days. You think you won't, but that is just Yankee bravado. Now about this diary."

That's what he was like: threatening and scholarly by turns. The diary seemed to obsess him; he kept coming back to it. "Now about this diary, you will sign a statement as to its truth. How do you know it speaks the truth? Because Mrs. Sanders told you."

I shook my head. "I won't sign it. I won't go against my country like that."

"You will sign it after you have written it in your own hand."

"I won't sign a fucking thing. Do what you like with me, I won't sign it. You're wasting your time."

Mohammed Nabi stood up and ordered the others to get moving. "It may take some time, but no matter, you will crawl at my feet and beg me to let you sign. Once we are in our camp, there will be all the time in the world. We can turn you into a blind, dead quadriplegic, a vegetable, a *thing*. Think about it, Yankee."

I was thinking about it. A quick, clean bullet in the head was one thing; this was another. For years I had faced death, but never anything like this, this horror he was quite capable of inflicting on me. I had to make them kill me if there was no other way out. And that, I thought, wasn't going to be so easy.

We continued to trek through the hills. This looked like country that hadn't seen a human being until the Moros came. Mohammed Nabi told the Moro to free my hands and take the rope from around my neck. But I felt no gratitude, because I knew he was saving me for better things. On toward afternoon a spotter plane flew over and they made me take cover when they threw themselves into the brush. I looked up at the light plane and saw the marking of the Philippine Air Force. The plane circled and flew away at leisurely speed.

It was getting dark when we went down into a deep gorge with a stream flowing out of a hole in the cliff wall. Other Moros were there, cooking over small fires that would be hard to see from the air. They stared at me and some came close to torment me, but Mohammed Nabi drove them away.

"Don't try to escape," he warned me. "There is nowhere you can go. You will sleep where the guards can see you. I want you to think about what we have discussed."

"What is there to discuss?"

"There is everything to discuss. You may be a foolish man, but not a stupid one, I think. Many Americans are both. I am neither foolish nor stupid. I am highly intelligent, and it is not simply my own opinion. In China I was given many tests and scored very high. Can you say the same?"

"I'm intelligent enough." I didn't want to make myself out to be more intelligent than he was. That would have been a mistake; he wanted to talk down to me. He was a strange character who had been conditioned more than educated. There was always the echo of other voices when he talked. Still and all, he wanted to argue, to reinforce his point of view.

"You are not truly intelligent or you would not be here," he said. "Is it that as an American you can't really believe that we hate you? It would seem so. Yet we do hate you and every day, in all parts of the world, we give you proof of it."

An argument was better than a beating. "A lot of us believe you," I said.

"Do you?"

"Yes, I do."

"Do you hate us?"

"Not individually. I find it hard to do that."

"That is a ridiculous attitude and politically unsound. We are taught to hate all Americans, the whining liberal as much as the mindless reactionary. Perhaps we hate the liberal more because he is an impediment to revolution in countries where it might succeed if the reactionaries were in control. Oppression of the masses is the surest path of revolution. For example, if Franklin D. Roosevelt had not become president in 1933, there would almost certainly have been a revolution. The masses would have risen up against their oppressors whose criminal manipulation of the economy had brought about the Great Depression. These same capitalists reviled Franklin D. Roosevelt and wished him dead, little realizing that he was in fact their savior. Without him, capitalism would have come to a bloody end in America. Instead, it staggered onward, propped up by the crippled villain's so-called social programs, his fascist demagoguery designed to convince the starving masses that conditions were not as bad as they appeared. Only be provoking the Japanese into an attack on Pearl Harbor, an attack that he knew was sure to come, did he manage to put America on an inflationary wartime economy. Can you deny any of this?"

He wanted an argument; I had to give him one; his half-savage companions didn't provide the "intellectual" give and take he longed for. He had come a long way from the rice paddy or wherever he worked before the Chinese got a hold of him. Or maybe he hadn't.

"Of course I can deny it," I said. "Your friend Karl Marx believed revolution would come first in the industrialized countries. It didn't happen that way, not even when there were no jobs and people were hungry. Sure the Communists marched and made speeches, but nothing happened. Where did revolution come? In the poor countries. Russia. China. More lately, Cuba. The industrialized countries that did go Communist had no choice in the matter. They got it as a gift. It came riding in on Russian tanks."

His dark eyes glittered; maybe my argument for our side had been too strong. The Moros, understanding none of it, watched us in silence. They looked attentive when Mohammed Nabl talked, scornful when I did. I felt like an unpopular fighter matched against a hometown boy with all his relatives rooting for him in the front row. No matter how good a show I put on, I wasn't going to get any applause.

Mohammed Nabi resumed the attack. "You display your ignorance when you state that Czarist Russia was not an industrialized country at the time of the revolution. There were many factories in eastern Russia. Have you forgotten the Trans-Siberian railway?"

I had forgotten the Trans-Siberian, but I wasn't ready to admit it. The penalty for forgetting might be death; Mohammed Nabi was that kind of guy. If it sounds funny now, it wasn't funny then. For the moment, I was a prisoner of this character's conceit. He could do anything he liked with me.

I said, "Russia was an economic mess when the revolution came along. Nothing worked. The soldiers they sent to fight the Germans were armed with rusty rifles that often blew up when there was enough ammunition to fire them. Mostly there wasn't. No food, no shoes. Morale was bad, leadership didn't exist. The Czarist government wasn't overthrown. It just collapsed. How can you call that a revolution?"

The Moros scowled at me; so did Mohammed Nabi. His scowl was so fierce the Moros thought it was time to work me over again. So did I, and I got ready for it. But it didn't come.

Mohammed Nabi poked the fire with a stick, sending up sparks. His dark face and glittering eyes reminded me of the wicked witch-doctor in the Tarzan movies, with one big difference: this guy made his bad medicine with an AK-47.

"Your words are a gross insult to the heroes of the revolution. Watch what you say or you will be severly punished."

Severely punished! I wondered what they'd been doing to me since he killed Freddy. If that wasn't punishment, then what could I expect when he really put his mind to it?

I didn't think it would do any good if I apologized to the heroes of the revolution. Nothing I did was going to score any points with this guy. He was a savage with a Marxist education; his personality was an uneasy balance of wild man and political robot; there seemed to be a constant struggle to keep himself under control. I wasn't sure he was completely sane.

The diary hadn't been mentioned for a while, but I knew he was thinking about it. So was I. It was the only reason I hadn't been killed. The tribesman in him wanted to kill me, to make me suffer before I died. Moros have a love, an appreciation, of torture that goes far beyond what we call sadism. For them, inflicting pain is an art that goes back for centuries, and among the tribes they tell stories of this or that legendary torturer, some pioneer of pain who devised some method no one had tried before. No doubt there were many failed experiments, times of disappointment and frustration when the subject died before the maximum effect could be achieved. But Rome wasn't built in a day; it took years before Alexander Graham Bell was able to say "Mary had a little lamb" over the telephone. Research is what does it.

Mohammed Nabi snapped his fingers. "Quick! Tell me what you are thinking about. Do not hesitate. Tell me!"

Daniel Boone once got away from his Indian captors by flapping his arms and squawking like a wild turkey. They were so astonished, he was able to make a break for it. I knew I couldn't hope to do anything as dramatic as that. Anyway, the redskins didn't have automatic rifles.

"I was thinking about Alexander Graham Bell. You know, the inventor of the telephone."

Mohammed Nabi made a scoffing sound. "What an undisciplined thing the American mind is! You face death and your only thoughts are of a fraud who lived a century ago. You should open your mind to knowledge in the short time you have left. Alexander Graham Bell did *not* invent the telephone. It was invented by Nicolai Simonov twenty years before the lying Scotsman stole his ideas."

Part of his Chinese education must have been reading *The Boy's Book of Knowledge.* You used to meet guys like him in the old regular army, cranky old soldiers who hadn't gone beyond the eighth grade and tried to make up for it by reading almanacs, quiz books, supermarket encyclopedias, *The Guinness Book of Records.* They could tell you everything you didn't need to know.

"So you say," I said.

"I do not say, I know." The Moro was as sure of that as he was of everything else. Global revolution was just around the corner, and he was going to be an important part of it. Excitement showed in his face when he talked of revolution; he had a hard-on for revolution. I never saw a guy who could get as excited about a political theory.

He dropped Alexander Graham Bell and went on to other things. I think he fancied himself a psychologist; maybe he'd taken courses at Won Ton University. That would figure: these days the Chinese washed brains instead of laundry. We learned that in Korea. I could see Mohammed Nabi interrogating prisoners in the underground cells of police stations. He'd be in full uniform, probably with major's insignia, and he'd have a better haircut. Now his hair was long and shaggy, bound up Apache style with a colored headband. He wore the headband under his Castro cap; it hung down the back of his neck.

He asked me questions that seemed to have no connection, and clicked his fingers when the answers didn't come fast enough. Some were political, some were sexual, all were idiotic. Was I aware that the Hollywood studios still controlled Ronald Reagan, as President? Did I know that Reagan had once been a Communist? Was Henry Kissinger queer? Was I queer? How could I honestly deny that all American men were queer? What was my current bank balance? In any given day, how much time did I spend watching television? Did I get a stiff dick when I thought about raping Russia with nuclear missiles?

They don't have game shows like that on television; the m.c.'s may be nasty, but their power to do harm is limited. This m.c. could cut my head off, and I didn't like the audience, either. He seemed to think he was making progress, this mental giant with the greasy face and the smell of sweat. The Moros listened, motionless, attentive, silent. It might go on for hours. I was battered and tired. I wanted to sleep.

The questions came faster and faster. The idea of brainwashing is to blank out the mind, to make it receptive to suggestion. But it has to be done right, the interrogator has to have infinite patience. This wild man didn't have it, though he tried hard enough. In the end, it all led back to the diary.

He took it out of a canvas bag and held it on both hands, like a preacher squeezing the Bible for emphasis. He seemed to find some significance in the moment. I looked at the leather-bound book, thinking of the man who had written it so many years before. Mrs. Sanders said it was fake; Mohammed Nabi wanted it to be real; I had no opinion because I hadn't read it.

The Moro opened the diary at random and held it down so he could read by the light of the fire. He flipped from one place to another. The Moros watched him, their leader of great learning. The firelight flickered in his face as he read. Now and then he looked up to see how I was reacting. Finally he closed the diary and thought for a while.

"There is no doubt in my mind that this is an authentic record," he said at last. "It cannot be otherwise. To call it a fake is a stupid or devious refusal to accept what is probable. Answer me."

"How can I? I haven't read it."

"I may give you a chance to read it. Will you give an honest answer if I do?"

"I'll give you an honest opinion."

"I doubt if you could be honest about anything. How could you? Your entire society is built on lies. However, here is the diary. Read it. I have read it several times. You may begin now."

He handed me the diary. There were stains on the cover, but it was in better condition than I expected. The waterproof case Sanders used must have been a good one. I opened it and looked at his large, bold handwriting. An expert might have decided that here was a man with a direct, forceful personality. All it meant to me was I could read it without any trouble.

"Proceed," Mohammed Nabi said.

I proceeded.

FOUR

Mohammed Nabi watched me through the flames of the fire while I read the first entry in General Sanders' diary.

Manila, July 29, 1941:
  War with Japan is imminent, and I do not see how it can be avoided. The Japanese make no secret of their determination to dominate all of Asia, yet the Washington politicians and the President himself continue to drag their feet on the vital matter of defending the Philippines against the coming onslaught. Surely the Philippines must be high on the list of Japanese invasion targets. These islands, less than 600 miles from the Asian mainland, are on the edge of the Western Pacific and a barrier to Japanese expansion in that area, and it is hard to see how they can take Asia without first taking the Philippines. Douglas MacArthur still believes the Philippines can be made into a "fortress" which would effectively block Japan's eastward thrust, but without a vast air and naval buildup—new bases, new airfields— how can this be done? I fail to see a solution. If we attempt to do it now, after delaying so long,

the Japanese will see it as a signal that we are preparing for war, and would attack posthaste. An attack will come, whatever we do, yet the pro-Independence politicians in Washington continue to put forward the idiotic idea that the Filipinos are capable of defending themselves. The Filipino leaders, for their part, insist that since the United States continues to occupy these islands, their defense is an American responsibility and a moral obligation. Hypocrites all, they say, "If you had granted us independence thirty or more years ago we would be a self-sufficient nation by now, with a strong army, navy and air force. We would have no need of American assistance." Pernicious rubbish, of course, and yet there is a grain of truth in it. To use a vulgar but pertinent expression, "We should have shit or got off the pot." Instead, we have gone along for decades, doing neither one, with the result that the Filipinos remain half subject and half free.

We should, like the British, who have more experience in such matters, have assumed complete responsibility for the defense of our "colony." Most Filipino leaders, so called, demand independence as a way to pleasing the mob, yet they don't really want it. A few, Jose Laurel and his followers, hate all white men and will welcome the Japanese with open arms when they come. There are traitors here, as there are at home, and it is my firm belief that many pro-Independence politicians and military planners are in the pay of powerful business interests who support Filipino independence only because they see it as a means to control these islands without having to answer to American public opinion. Some men betray their country out of political conviction. Others do it for profit.

This was Sanders' first reference to homegrown "traitors," but the word "treason" and "traitor" were sprinkled throughout the diary.

Men, famous and abscure, appeared in its pages like characters in a play. MacArthur had the lead, but Sanders himself had second billing as the narrator and the hero's most trusted friend. Sanders, it seemed, was not blind to his hero's shortcomings, but they were always excused as the tiny flaws which all great men possess. In Sanders' view, Mac was too Olympian, too above it all, to deal effectively with the villains in Manila and Washington.

"Douglas takes the long view of history," one entry read, *"while what it needed at this moment is a commander-in-chief who will kick their teeth in."*

The next entry, dated a week later, told of the beginnings of the conspiracy to take over the Philippines: to make them free for a take-over by greedy businessmen in the States. It read:

Manila, August 7, 1941:

On Tuesday, while in the officers' club at Camp Frame, I was having a drink with Major Wilbur C. Coakley, when he brought up the subject of Philippine independence, a not uncommon topic of discussion among Americans in these islands. I was not prepared to engage in yet another examination of this irritating subject, and was rather blunt in my response.

"What is there to discuss," I said, or words to that effect. "It's going to be the ruination of these islands, but what can we do about it?"

Coakley then said in what seemed to me a rather furtive manner, "It need not be, Colonel. Independence will come, we all know, and it certainly presents a problem for the Filipinos, although they don't know it yet. Most of us who have served here for any length of time love these islands and their simple people and their abandonment by the United States disturbs us. They are vital to America's interest, but Washington doesn't seem to think so. Only a few years ago, the British and the Dutch were ready to move in if we moved out. The war with Germany scotched that idea."

I was in no mood to be lectured on recent history by a subordinate; I told him to get to the point. Once again there was that furtive look and he said, "Suppose Philippine independence could be guaranteed by some outside force?"

Somewhat testily I replied, "The only outside force coming here will be the Japanese. We all know there is a war coming, and we'll win it, of course, bu that will take years. Meanwhile, the Japanese will control these islands."

"Not necessarily, sir," Coakley said confidently. "If the United States pulls out, the Japanese probably won't see the Philippines as any kind of threat, especially if the islands are governed by men who will remain neutral even if there is a war between the U.S. and Japan. Germany hasn't attacked Sweden or Switzerland or Eire, has it? Why? Because they are not a threat to Germany's aims. But the U.S. will have to pull out of the Philippines lock, stock and barrel before the islands are safe from a Japanese invasion."

I thought this was a most peculiar opinion, coming from a serving American officer as it did, but in my response I said nothing to dissuade him from continuing.

"You may speak freely, Major," I said. "Tell me, what is this outside force? Businessmen who have a great deal of money invested here? If so, it is quite understandable."

There must have been something in my voice to make him wary despite my encouragement to speak his mind, because immediately he backtracked and said that what he had been setting forth was simply a theory and not necessarily his own assessment of the situation.

"But it's entirely within the realm of possibility," he said pompously. "After independence, American capital and the right kind of pressure could bring about governmental solvency and social stability. In theory, at least, there need be no conflict of interest even if the U.S. and Japan go to war, just as long as the Philippines remain neutal."

At this point I was inclined to add, "You mean, neutral in favor of Japan, in the same way that Britain was neutral in favor of the Confederacy." However, this would not have been wise, however cutting it might have been, so I merely nodded and said, "Well, it's something to think about, isn't it. We ought to discuss it again sometime."

"Any time you'd like to, sir," Coakley said a little too eagerly, I thought.

Here we were joined by other officers and the matter was dropped. I went home.

That night, according to Sanders, he thought long and hard about what Coakley had said. It was no casual conversation, he concluded, and much more than a theory.

"Suddenly, idle gossip overheard and forgotten, began to take on a sinister shape in my mind," Sanders wrote. "Because of boredom, I suppose, all foreign posts are hotbeds of malicious chitchat, but I knew intuitively that something was going on that had nothing to do with clubhouse whispers. For a moment, I wondered if Coakley might be working for army intelligence, had been sent to sound me out, then I recalled that throughout his career, from West Point on, he had been known far and wide as a 'politician,' that is, an officer who seeks advancement by means of political and social influence. I recalled, too, that he was married to

59

the niece of Baylor Johnston, a San Francisco businessman with extensive sugar holdings in central Luzon. Of course, this was no indictment of Johnston, nor even to Coakley, but I resolved to discover everything I could, and then bring the entire matter to Douglas MacArthur's attention. Coakley, I felt sure, would, in time, lead me to the higher-ups, provided that such traitors really did exist. I hoped, for the sake of the Philippines, that they did not.

Thus ended the second entry in General Sanders' diary. A lot had been packed into just a few pages, maybe too much; even so, I wasn't ready to write it off as a lie. The way he put it down, without wild accusations, hung together pretty well. You didn't have to be a historian to know that the big American investors tried their damnedest to hold onto the Philippines. Independent native governments drive big businessmen up the wall; they try, whenever possible, to preserve the status quo. But that didn't make them part of a conspiracy, as Sanders seemed to think. Neither did it prove them innocent. As Sanders said to Coakley, it was something to think about.

I looked up and saw Mohammed Nabi watching me from the other side of the fire. Our eyes locked for a moment, then he smiled and told one of the guards to give me food. I ate quickly, stringy roast chicken and sweet tea, and went back to my reading.

The next entry was dated August 18, 1941. Sanders wrote:

Met Coakley and Colonel Noel Parsons in the Camp Frame club tonight. I hadn't encountered

Parsons before since he had been in the islands for less than a month. He is much less affable than Coakley, but much more intelligent, I think. It turned out that Parsons knows a great deal about the Philippines through reading and family connections: his grandfather served as a captain during the Philippine Insurrection, and his uncle, a retired lumberman, still lives in the mountain resort town of Baguio, which in the Philippines, has the same posh social standing as Asheville has in North Carolina.

I asked Parsons what his uncle thought of Philippine independence and, surprisingly enough, he replied that his uncle thought it inevitable and would be most welcome when it came, for he (Parsons' uncle) intended to become a citizen of the new Philippine Republic the moment it became a reality.

According to Parsons, his uncle felt that since he had spent his life in the islands, and had grown rich there, he owed the country a debt of allegiance. Coakley then asked me if I had given any further thought to our conversation of August 7, and I replied that I had considered his theory with interest, since I, too, owned some property in Mindanao, purchased for next to nothing in 1936, and hoped to see it increase in value someday.

In reply, Coakley said it was sure to, once the country was fully developed, but that that was possible only when the economy and the government were stabilized.

(Again that word "stabilized!")

Here, Parsons said many Americans were sure to relinquish their U.S. citizenship and become naturalized Filipinos once independence was granted. The Filipinos were going to need American know-how, Parsons said, plus a core of ex-U.S. Army officers to run their armed forces until they learned to do it themselves, and from his manner and tone of voice, he suggested that this was going to take a great many

61

years.

I said I thought that was what we had been doing all along, since 1901, in fact, but Parsons said what he meant was a core of ex-officers, former American citizens, who intended to spend the rest of their lives in the islands, not as temporary advisors but as a fully integrated part of Philippine society.

"Americans, former Americans, would control the country much more completely than we do now?" I ventured. I asked the question because I felt sure I would get a straight answer from Parsons. "A sort of American dictatorship, in fact?"

Parsons smiled at the word "dictatorship," saying it was too harsh. "But why not?" he said, smiling, one man of the world to another. "Look at it this way, Colonel," he continued. "What would the Philippines be like today if we hadn't rescued the country from the brutality and mismanagement of the Spaniards? We wiped out cholera, not the least of our achievements, and I don't know how many other diseases. We built hospitals and schools and roads and railroads and bridges. We deepened and improved their harbors, taught, or tried to teach, a sensible system of agriculture. We smashed the hold the Moro pirates had on the southern islands. Before we came, the Philippine islands were just eight thousand islands, half of them even without names. Today, the people here have a country."

Smiling too, I said, "Waiting to be plucked from the tree by American businessmen?"

"You are too cynical, sir," Parsons replied, his manner indicating that he meant no offense. "American businessmen have been here for forty years and the country has prospered. It will prosper even more if everything is done more efficienctly. You know as well as I do that the Filipinos aren't ready for complete independence, but being a childishly proud people, they like the sound of it."

Yes, I agreed, they liked the sound of it.

"Think of it another way," Parsons went on. "For four decades one of the principal Filipino complaints has been that Americans have held themselves aloof from the life of the country. Filipinos, except for the top political leaders, were barred from our clubs, our places of recreation. Unlike the Spaniards, we never took Filipino wives. Mistresses, certainly, but never wives."

"And you would change all that?" I asked.

"We would encourage change," Parsons answered. "There would be no social barriers except for those on the lowest levels of society."

"An interesting idea," I agreed. "Everything you've said is interesting."

"Yes, Colonel, but are you interested in becoming a part of it?" Parsons asked. "Before you answer, sir, let me say that you would not have been asked if I did not think that you are in sympathy with us. You don't have to give your answer now, just let me say that what I propose is not just the wild scheme of a few dreamers, and will never come to pass. Think about it, sir, that is all I ask you to do. If your answer is no, and I hope it is not, then we will say no more about it. I'm sure we can trust your discretion."

I said I would think about it.

Mohammed Nabi ordered one of the guards to build up the fire; I went on reading. Most of the Moros were asleep. Only Mohammed Nabi and the night guards remained awake, watching me as I turned the pages of this incredible journal. Mohammed Nabi drank many cups of sweet tea and chainsmoked his brown paper cigarettes. Sometimes the night wind gusted up, blowing the fire my way, but I was hardly aware of it. I had come a long way to find a fake diary, and now I wasn't sure of anything. Major

Coakley's name meant nothing to me, but I knew, from the newspapers, that Colonel Noel Parsons was still alive, quite old now but still active in Republican politics in Southern California. He was a king-maker, the papers said: one of the immensely wealthy men who really ruled America.

I had seen him on television, one of the keynote speakers at some Republican convention, and it was hard to link him to the "traitor" described by Sanders. He had retired a famous major general after World War II and gone into business. What business? I couldn't remember. Would a man like that, a super patriot, be ready to betray his country for money and power? I had no answer for that. At the moment, I had no answer for anything.

I read on and other names began to appear: Congressman (now Senator) Cy McCausland (D) of Texas; Evan Evans, the "legendary" real estate developer from New York; Morris Silverhorn, the "celebrity" public relations whiz, who was said to have sold food freezers to the Eskimos and had managed the campaign of at least one President. Silverhorn was dead, killed in a plane crash, but the others were very much alive. To know that, all you had to do was to read the newsmagazines. I could see where Sanders might have something against a Congressman, but why would he want to smear a real estate man and a publicist? This, I thought, was where Mrs. Sanders' story about the general's "enemies" fell apart. Maybe not: it could be a clever way to make the whole thing look good.

I turned to the next page dated August 30, 1941.

Hotel McKinley, Manila:
Now that I have been accepted into this traitorous cartel, Noel Parsons took me to a meeting at the McKinley Hotel. Previously, he had spoken to McCausland, Evans and Silverhorn as being important members, and now here they were in the flesh. Also present, though he wasn't mentioned earlier, was Matsuoka Haro, a ranking official of the Japanese Foreign Service. Everyone was slightly uneasy at first, but the atmosphere grew more cordial after everyone had a few drinks. (The Japanese had one drink, and so did I.) Finally, we—or they—got down to business, and what was said there made my hair stand on end, so to speak. The gist of the meeting was that McCausland would continue to drum up support for Philippine independence by every means available to him, and if that meant the hiring of private detectives and political blackmail, then so be it.

"I don't even think that will be necessary," McCausland said. "I can count on men in the House and Senate, but because I'm just a freshman Congressman, I have to be the point man, the one that takes the heat if anything goes wrong."

McCausland went on to say that his "friends" in the Congress would do everything in their power to prevent a war with Japan, even if it meant making unpopular concessions in the Far East. Britain would have to go it alone, McCausland declared, saying that a British defeat was none of America's business.

"We have no intention in getting into a war with our friend Japan," McCausland said. "At the moment, the Philippines are a sore point between our two countries. However, this friction will cease to exist the moment we withdraw our forces and the country becomes a neutral republic."

This extraordinary statement was hailed by Matsuoka Haro, who said it was a giant step toward repairing relations, strained at the moment, between his country and Congressman McCausland's. Japan had no designs on the Philippines, now or in the future.

After these pleasantries were out of the way, Morris Silverhorn reported that his pro-Independence public relations campaign was going extremely well in the States.

Evan Evans, the realtor, said financing was no problem: the group he was associated with was prepared to provide almost unlimited funding provided they were given "first crack" at developing all the likely resort areas in the islands.

Colonel Parsons said that had already been agreed upon. "You don't have to take just my word for it, Mr. Evans," he said. "The guarantee comes right from the top."

(The top? I wondered. Where was the top? Who was the top?)

The meeting lasted little more than an hour. I never saw McCausland, Evans or Silverhorn again. Colonel Parsons, who had more than enough to drink, "persuaded" me to accompany him to the hotel bar, where he continued to drink.

"I'm glad you came in with us," he told me after a while, "because I like you and know you're a good man. You got in on the ground floor and there will come a time when you'll come to me and say, 'I owe it all to you, Noel my friend. I tell you, we can't miss. The Filipinos may put up a bit of a squawk, but all that's been worked out. A few people may get clobbered, but that can't be helped. You can't make an omelette without cracking eggs. We'll be in the driver's seat before the little brown bastards know what's happening."

I had to take Colonel Parsons home in a taxi.

Sanders' next entry was made on September 22, 1941. It read:

This morning I took my findings to Douglas MacArthur and he listened in his usual impassive manner, then said quite simply, "I don't want to hear any more about it. That is all."

For once, I attempted to argue with him, to make him see the truth of my accusations; all he did was repeat, "That is all, you are dismissed."

I read that entry again, trying to visualize the scene between the two men, one imperial and aloof, the other trying to keep his temper and barely making it. It "played," as actors say, because MacArthur was the kind of man who could never admit that a conspiracy was taking shape right under his nose. What he didn't know didn't exist, or if it did, it wasn't of much importance.

If the diary could be believed, and I was beginning to believe it, Sanders was bitterly disappointed by MacArthur's frosty reaction; he was an angry man, but he wasn't mad at the guy with the crushed cap and the corncob pipe. In the entries that followed his brief meeting with MacArthur, he raged against the conspirators, trying to make up his mind about what he should do. These entries were interesting only because of the picture they gave of Sanders himself. He wondered if he should go to army intelligence and decided that would be disloyal to Big Mac.

"Besides," he wrote, *"they might not believe me, might even consider me deranged, and that*

would be the end of my career. My strongest inclination is to resign from the army, but how can I do that when Douglas MacArthur needs me? There are bad days ahead and so I must remain in the service of my country."

For all his bitterness and anger, or because of it, Sanders continued his association with the men he called "those swinish traitors, those Benedict Arnolds in high places," and additional names were named, including a brigadier general, a powerful Filipino senator high up in the *Nacionalista* Party; a U.S. Navy submarine commander; and a former and unofficial advisor to President Roosevelt. This went on all through November of 1941, and at one point, late in the month, Sanders wrote: *"For all their careful planning, for all their wealth, connections and power, they are worried as war grows ever closer in spite of their best efforts to prevent it. Their dream of empire is so close they can't believe that it may slip from their sweaty hands. I know it's sinful to pray for war, but that's what I do. War, in a way, would put an end to all this."*

It did.

On December 7, 1941, the Japs bombed Pearl Harbor.

The rest of the bulky diary dealt with Sanders' war experiences, his promotion to brigadier general, his service in Korea, his decision to resign after MacArthur was fired. I read the last page and closed the leatherbound book. I knew it wasn't a fake. Mrs. Sanders had been lying. I looked across the fire at Mohammed Nabi and he was smiling, but nothing was said just then. I sat there, wanting time to think. It didn't

68

matter what the diary was; I still had the problem of how to stay alive. Finally Mohammed Nabi said, "You didn't eat much, do you want more food?"

I said yes and the guard gave it to me. I ate stringy chicken, chewing every bite like you're supposed to, wondering what the hell I was going to do. I could try to make a run for it and hope they'd kill me, but I knew that wasn't going to happen. They would run me down and tie me hand and foot. Sure as hell, I wasn't going to sign anything. Then would come the torture. Maybe Mohammed Nabi would leave that till morning.

I was going over other unpleasant ideas when Mohammed Nabi stood up and said, "Well, Yankee, you've read the general's diary from cover to cover. What do you think of it?"

"It's a phony," I said.

FIVE

Mohammed Nabi had learned English in China, and was fluent in a stiff sort of way, but it didn't include slang words like "phony." Failing to understand, he became dangerous in an instant.

"What did you say, Yankee?"

"I said the diary is a fake, a fraud. There isn't a word of truth In It. I already told you the old man made it up to get revenge on his enemies."

Mohammed Nabi came around the fire, followed by the two AK-47-toting guards. They grinned at me, hoping to see some pain inflicted. They were all set to work me over, but Mohammed Nabi stopped them with a snap of his finger. His eyes regarded me with infinite contempt.

"You are a lying fool," he said. "Everything in the diary is true. I could see it in your eyes as you read it. You tried to conceal it, but there were moments when it showed through. I can tell, I have been trained to tell truth from lies. And you, Yankee, are lying."

The son of a bitch wanted the diary to be the real thing, was so convinced of its authenticity that he was ready to do anything to prove his point. Having his opinion questioned made his black eyes glitter with cruelty.

"The diary is a fake," I repeated.

He forced himself to be calm. "Is there any way you can prove what you are saying?"

"Not without Mrs. Sanders to back me up. She told me it was a fake and I believe her. Why should an old woman lie about the contents of her dead husband's diary?"

"Because she has been threatened by some of the men named in the diary. They have threatened to kill her if the book isn't recovered and destroyed. That is the reason she lied to you. You were not supposed to believe what was in it."

"If these men who threatened her know about the book, then why didn't they send their own agents to get it?"

Mohammed Nabi slapped my face, but it was a love tap compared to what I had been through earlier. Yeah, he's going to torture me, I thought, and he wants me fully awake when he does it.

He thought for a moment, trying to get his Marxist logic together. Then he said, "Perhaps you are one of their agents?"

"You keep changing your mind," I said. "First you said I was CIA, now I'm a hired thug in the pay of traitors."

He thought he had me there. He was intelligent, but his mental processes weren't too well oiled. "Then you *know* they are traitors?"

"You said that, not me." That should have

earned me another slap. It didn't.

He tried another tack; this time it was bribery. I guess the Chinese had convinced him that all Americans were dumb as well as evil. "Rainey," he said, "there is no need for any of this. When we first captured you, you told me you were a mercenary, a soldier of fortune. Well, I cannot approve of such a profession, but after all what you do is not my concern. We are fighting the government of Ferdinand Marcos, and the Americans are only indirectly involved. I repeat, our fight is against the Filipinos, not the Americans. Do you follow my reasoning?"

I nodded.

"Very well then," he went on, the lunatic bastard. "It took twenty thousand dollars that was to have gone for the purchase, the ransoming, of the diary. Now I am prepared to return the money—we have all the money we need—and to set you free, to give you back your life, provided you admit that the diary is authentic."

"How do I know you'll keep your word?" I wanted to know.

"Because there is nothing to be gained by killing you. All you have to do is nod and we will take you to the coast. You will be richer by twenty thousand dollars and no one will ever know about it."

I took a deep breath. "The diary is a fake," I said, knowing that I wasn't going to get any more offers.

Marxist or not, I think he was glad the question and answer session was at an end. He wanted the glory of having recovered an invaluable piece of anti-American information. Just he same, he was a Moro and cruelty was second nature to him. He spoke to the guards and they took hold of me, but there were no more slaps, not even a hard shove. They stripped off my clothes and tied me to a tree. One of them tied my penis with a piece of string, so tight that red spots of pain danced in front of my eyes.

"Now we will fill you full of water," Mohammed Nabi said calmly. "We will keep pouring water into you until your bladder bursts. That will take some time and the agony can't even be imagined. To stop it, all you have to do is to tell the truth."

Talk, you stupid son of a bitch, I told myself. What the fuck does it matter? Talk and you'll get a quick bullet through the head. I was still fighting with myself when someone came running and there was a babble of words. The only one I understood was "radio."

Suddenly I found myself unbound, my penis untied. The pain was so great that I would have fallen to the ground if the guards hadn't caught me in time. The water that was to have been forced down my throat was now being poured over my throbbing dick. Then the sons of bitches carried me to the fire and covered me with a blanket. A bottle was held to my mouth and I drank from it. Whatever it was, it was good and strong and I gagged before I got used to it and drank as much as I could. By the time they took the bottle away I was feeling no pain in more than one respect. I lay back gasping.

It doesn't take long to get drunk if you drink about half a pint of liquor in one go. Mohammed Nabi's face was bent over me and I tried to kick it as hard as I could. He pulled back, but didn't go away. I think he looked worried.

"What the fuck is going on here?" I yelled up at him. "You fucking sadist, what do you think you're doing? Answer up, you donkey driver, before I cut your fucking throat!"

I don't know what else I called him, but it must have been plenty. "Calm yourself, Rainey," he said soothingly. "Sleep and we will talk later. There will be no more pain."

Drunk as I was, I heard the anger behind his soft words. Something had happened to change things, but what it was, I had no way of knowing. I tried to think and found it impossible. I went to sleep.

When I woke up it was still dark and I was still under the blanket. Mohammed Nabi squatted beside me, the bottle in his hand, wanting to know if I needed another drink. Overhead the Asian sky was full of stars.

"Water," I said.

Mohammed Nabi put the bottle aside and held a canteen to my mouth. The water in it was fresh and cold and tasted better than anything I could remember. Sober now, I could only wonder that I was still alive when all the odds said I should be dead. The stars were bright, but I could tell it was getting on toward morning.

"What happened to the water torture?" I said, thinking I'd never be right if I didn't kill this man.

"There will be no more of that," he answered. "My orders are to bring you to regional command. What happened was a mistake, but I had no orders to the contrary."

75

I remembered the single word "radio" I was able to understand through the babble and the pain. "You got your new orders by radio?"

"Yes," he said, apparently too worried to ask how I knew. "Regional command said you were to be taken there for questioning."

"I didn't know I was that important."

"You must be very important, or regional command would not have ordered me to bring you there. My orders are that you are not to be harmed in any way. Will you tell them that I mistreated you?"

I was beginning to think he really was crazy when I realized he was nothing but a peasant with a quickly applied Marxist veneer that kept coming unglued. Like they say: you can take the boy out of Mindanao, but you can't take Mindanao out of the boy. He longed so hard for the approval of his Communist masters; now he was afraid and ashamed because he thought he had let them down.

"All they have to do is look at me to see I was mistreated," I said. "Why did you do it?"

"I had no orders to the contrary," he said. "When they radioed that you had been sent to Mindanao to recover the diary, all I was ordered to do was to find the diary before you did. I did find it. I had no orders about you. You were not important at that time. Then when I was called to the radio, they told me how important you were without explaining why they thought so. All they said on the radio was that the old woman who sent you had been killed and you must be captured and brought to regional command and not to be harmed on the way."

It was hard to keep the surprise out of my

voice. "Mrs. Sanders has been murdered?"

"That is what regional command told me. My friend the radio operator told me. We are both from the same village."

Well, there it was: the old lady had been knocked off and I was on my way to what Mohammed Nabi called "regional command." Somebody had killed the lying old broad, but one guess was as good as another. Who had done her in? President Marcos' secret police? A hired killer working for one of the "traitors" named in the diary? Maybe, I thought, it was just a burglar.

I asked Mohammed Nabi and he said regional command hadn't given him that information.

"How did regional command know about the diary?" I asked.

"They didn't tell me," he repeated like a fucking parrot.

The housekeeper? I asked myself. Who else could it be? No one else knew I was coming to Manila, or why. No one else had the opportunity to eavesdrop while I was talking to Mrs. Sanders. I voted for the housekeeper because she was the only candidate on the ticket. Her betrayal might not be intentional; someone in her family, if she had a family, might be a member of the Philippine Communist Party or one of its militant arms, the People's Liberation Army, the National Liberation Front. A whispered confidence in the wrong ear, this or that, who could tell? Or, to keep it simple, she might have sold the information to the Communists for a few dollars. Few things happen by accident: there's usually a motive.

"It will not be good for you when we reach regional command," Mohammed Nabi said, as if talking to himself.

Tough shit, I thought; things would be even worse for him if I could get to him first. "How can they blame you for what happened?" I said. "You had no orders to the contrary."

"True," he agreed. "But regional command will not care about that. We are taught to anticipate trouble and to avoid it. But I am glad you weren't dead when I was called to the radio. That is something in my favor."

"Mine too," I said, thinking that of all the weird characters I'd met in my time, this one was probably the weirdest. "I suppose I can expect to be treated well from here on in?"

Mohammed Nabi nodded solemnly. "You will be treated very well. There is nothing to worry about."

Like hell there wasn't. Just the same, I was alive and anything could happen on the way. Always look on the bright side, I always say.

"We will start as soon as you dress in your new clothes," Mohammed Nabi said. "I took your measurements while you slept. We have supplies and extra clothing here. At least your clothes will not look as if they have been mistreated. That, too, will be in my favor."

He handed me Cuban Army fatigues, shirt, boots, socks, belt, Fidel Castro cap, and I got dressed. By the time I finished, the sun was coming up and the men were cooking breakfast. I got some kind of Moro pancakes smeared with honey and more of that sweet tea. As I ate, the Moros looked at me with an interest that hadn't been there before. Last night all I'd been was a miserable American foreigner to be kicked and spat on; now I was being taken to give a regional command performance. Still eating, I turned to look at the tree where I had been tied and found it hard to suppress a shudder. In a few minutes it was time to move out.

The hills began to turn into mountains. Sixty percent of the Philippines is mountainous, with hills and very few flat places in between. The mountain we were climbing was thick with tropical growth; once there had been rice terraces here, but now they had been abandoned, their peasant proprietors scared off by the war. The country, especially in the south, is hot and wet, and it rained before we had been on the march for half an hour. Then the rain stopped and the green mountain steamed in the morning sun. It went on like that for several hours: sudden downpours followed by sun and steam. You sweated like a pig, then you got a bath, then you sweated again.

We crossed the top of the mountain, went down into a narrow, swampy valley that once had contained rice paddies, then started to climb an even higher mountain on the far side. Climbing up through the rain forest that clung to the side of this mountain, I saw snakes, a lot of striped snakes slithering in the wet brush. The Moros paid no attention to them, and neither did I, though I watched where I put my feet. Mohammed Nabi saw what I was doing, so I asked him if the snakes were poisonous.

"Very deadly, but few snakes are aggressive," he told me. "You are safe, Rainey: the men ahead of you scare them off. You will not die of snakebite before you reach regional command."

Now it was "Rainey" all the way; no more "Yankee," or "capitalist running dog," or "fascist pig," or any of the other names he had called me in the early stages of our friendship. I half expected him to ask me to put in a good word for him at regional command; that would have been too much, even for him. But the vicious, confused son of a bitch couldn't have been nicer; he was scared shitless of what regional command might do to him for his mistreatment of an important prisoner who had some of the important answers they wanted. A more experienced guerrilla would have known better; this one had been given a command and sent into the wilds where the only people he had to deal with were frightened farmers. In a "civilized" Communist country his bosses might yell at him, but they'd hardly shoot him. But this was the Philippines, so maybe he had good reason to be shaking in his shoes.

We crossed the second mountain and stopped to eat on the downward slope, and it was hotter in the shade of the trees than out in the sun. It had just rained on that side of the mountain and the air was full of water. None of that bothered the Moros; nothing appeared to bother them. Mohammed Nabi frowned and mumbled to himself, but he was the exception. His wonderful career was going down in flames and he felt bad about it. I looked at the AK-47's and thought, now if only I could get my hands on one of those babies. One of the Moros carried a light machine gun and was very proud of being given so much responsibility. The humid climate of the island is hell on weapons and every time we stopped to rest, he wiped the light gun off with an oily rag, looking for rust spots that weren't there. He grinned at me when he saw me looking at the light gun, then he patted the barrel with pride of ownership and shook his head. Look but don't touch, was his message to me.

"The Moros are a very proud people," Mohammed Nabi said, as if we had been discussing the subject.

"So I've been told," I said.

"It's true," he said. "We were in these islands before the Spaniards. Time after time they invaded Mindanao and Sulu, but we always drove them out. We destroyed the army led by Esteban Rodriquez de Rigueroa in 1596. I will have to admit that they captured Zamboanga in 1636, but they paid a heavy price for it. Our counterattack was ferocious, bloody and terrible. No matter how hard they tried, the Spanish could never conquer us. Do you doubt me, Rainey?"

"Not for a minute," I said, more interested in the AK-47's than in this disappointed fanatic's history lesson.

"In the nineteenth century, Moro pirates still ruled the southern seas. We used forty- to one-hundred-ton war boats to raid far from the Philippines. They carried crews of fifty or sixty men and struck terror into all who had the misfortune to see them. Today, the Moros are as feared as they were in those days. There are many Communist groups in these islands, but the Moros of Mindanao and Sulu are the best fighters for socialist democracy. Marcos, the swine, has concentrated fifty thousand soldiers and police in the southern islands and has accomplished nothing. Those beautiful islands are our ancient strongholds and will remain so to the end of time."

He was carrying on so much about the past glories of his people that I wondered if he was contemplating suicide. He rattled off names and numbers, the dates of ancient battles. The Moros had been fighting outsiders for four hundred years and were ready to fight on for another four hundred. A thousand years, if necessary. Moro Pride, I thought. I could see it lettered on a tee-shirt.

He was telling me what a terrible fellow he was, personally, when his spiel was cut short by the rattle of gunfire somewhere up on the next mountain. He and his men were in no danger where they were, but the moment the distant shooting started he sprang into action, as he might say himself and probably would. But I guess he saw a furious firefight as a sure, probably the only way to redeem himself, to give his sagging career a much needed lift. "I cannot endanger your life, Rainey, so you must stay here under guard," he said to me. "One man will watch over you, but he will be armed with the light machine gun. If there are others and they come up the slope, the light machine gun will cut them to pieces. I am sorry, but I must tie your hands and feet. Those are government troops over there. They have cornered some of our people and we must go to help them."

There was nothing to do but let myself be roped. After it was done, he put my back against a tree so I wouldn't be too uncomfortable. "Regional command will hear what we did here today," he said. "Then things will not be so bad for me."

Mohammed Nabi and the Moros disappeared into the trees and suddenly it was quiet. The shooting on the far mountain hadn't started up again. I looked at the light machine gunner and he grinned at me. He was a young man, but his front teeth were rotting. He grinned a second time, then took the oily rag from his pocket after setting up the light gun so it faced the slope. He watched me while he polished the light gun with loving care. It was hot and the trees dripped. It was so quiet that I could hear the drops of water hitting the ground. No sound came from the slope, none from far away.

The gunner took a can of oil from his pocket and freshened his rag with a few drops. Then he screwed the top on tight and put the can away. Every time a drop of water from the trees fell on the light gun, he wiped it away. Every drop was an enemy, something to be hated and feared. There wasn't a sound.

An hour dragged by and nothing happened; it didn't even rain. If the counterinsurgency government troops had moved away fast, I hoped Mohammed Nabi wouldn't take it into his crazy head to follow them way back in the mountains. The ropes were cutting into my wrists, which were swelling painfully, and I didn't want to spend the whole day tied like that on the side of a stinking mountain. Besides—an even worse thought—there was a chance that Mohammed Nabi and his men might be wiped out in an ambush. The Moros despised the government troops, and while many of them might be pretty green, some of these anti-guerrilla units were known to be damned good at what they did. If my friend Mohammed Nabi got zapped, then I was far up shit creek: without orders, the light machine gunner might hang on here for days while I developed gangrene in my hands and feet. There was no way I could communicate with the guy, no way I could tell him that we ought to get off this mountain. All he would do is grin and keep on wiping his light gun with the oily rag.

Suddenly there was the rattle of automatic weapons from what seemed like miles away. It was so faint that I had to strain my ears to hear it. Now and then it faded, then resumed. The Moro guarding me grinned and pretended to fire his light gun. He made machine-gun noises with his mouth, the way American kids used to do when they came out of a war movie. He was still playing the fool when I saw the snake hanging down from the branch just over his head. The snake was black with yellow bands; its evil head moved this way or that. There was nothing aggressive in the way its head moved and maybe it was just curious, drawn there by the unfamiliar sounds the gunner was making.

I couldn't speak a word of the guy's language, but a shout would get his attention. But then the snake was sure to strike. The Moro continued to make his strange noises, but the snake didn't pull back. I looked at the snake and saw deliverance, provided I was willing to take the chance of rotting on the side of this mountain. I was ready to take the chance, so I screamed. The Moro sprang to his feet and the snake struck him on the back of the neck. Then it dropped from the tree and vanished into the brush. The moment the Moro, already a dead man, saw the snake, he screamed as loud as I had. He knew he'd be dead in minutes and he wanted to take me with him. Screaming and screaming, he pulled a knife from his belt and started toward me. The knife glinted dully in the shadows under the trees. Already there was a glazed look in the Moro's eyes, his legs were turning to rubber, but he kept coming with a fierce determination to kill the man who had killed him. There was nothing I could do to stop him: if he could make it across another few yards of ground, then I was as dead as he was.

He swayed on his feet, his mouth working soundlessly, maybe praying to Allah to give him the strength to finish the job. I looked up at him, but I don't think he could see me any longer. Then with one last terrible scream he threw himself forward, trying to plunge the knife into what he couldn't see. The knife came down close to my face and the dead man came with it, knocking the wind out of me. I smelled his sweat and his rotting teeth and I lay still for a moment with his body on top of me, then gathering all my strength, I rolled the corpse away. The corpse went, the knife stayed. It was quiet again except for the rasp of my breath and the rattle of far-off gunfire that went on and on.

Sitting on the ground, I backed into the knife until my numbed fingers cut themselves on the razor-sharp blade. I opened my hands and let the ropes move up and down against the blade, cutting myself when I misjudged the position of the blade. There was the trickle of blood, but absolutely no pain. Then the ropes parted and my hands were free. I rubbed my bleeding hands together, trying to restore the circulation, before I pulled the knife out of the ground and cut the ropes that bound my ankles. Jesus Christ! I thought. I have a chance now. I have a light machine gun and a knife, so that gives me a chance. I felt like yelling, but of course I didn't.

I was checking out the light gun when the shooting in the distance faltered, then stopped altogether. I waited for it to start up again. It didn't.

I didn't know how long it would take them to get back, if they got back, but I had to get set up, one way or another. If they all came back, I didn't stand much of a chance of surviving: the AK-47, like the M-16, is a machine rifle and not a submachine gun. It's a better, more dependable weapon than the M-16, and while I was in Vietnam, every guy I knew was trying to get hold of one. It has a terrific rate of fire; it shoots through mud or blood or mashed potatoes.

The light gun was a Chinese copy of the Soviet Katrinka, a fine weapon with a high rate of fire. I checked it over again and blessed the dead Moro for keeping it in such good working condition. No rust, no dirt anywhere I looked. It was belt fed and that can cause jamming problems except when you have a second man to watch the feed, but I'd never heard of any such problems with the Katrinka. Just one man could fire it efficiently unless he did something really stupid. It still wasn't any match for a whole bunch of AK-47's. All I could do was give it a try.

After I rolled the dead man into the brush, I went down the slope and looked back up at the light gun. The Moro had set it up well enough, but there was room for improvement, so I went back up and moved it to a better position. There wasn't much more I could do but wait. I thought of running and decided against it, because if only a few of them got back, they would hunt me through the mountains. They were the home folks and I was the stranger; they would catch me in no time at all, and having caught me, they would kill me in the worst possible way. I had killed one of their brothers; nothing Mohammed Nabi could do or say would get me a reprieve for that. So it was die now, maybe, or die later for sure.

I drank water from the dead man's canteen. It rained several times during the early afternoon, then it steamed as usual. I listened to the birds croaking in the trees, I kept an eye out for snakes with yellow bands on black bodies. Then suddenly the birds flew away and I knew they were coming. How many? I didn't know, I couldn't see them yet.

I lay down behind the light gun and got ready to kill. Now I could hear them coming up the slope. How many? I still couldn't see. Then I saw the first of them, then all of them: Mohammed Nabi walking at the head of only five men. Jesus Christ! I still had a chance, a God damned fine chance, and I wasn't going to screw it up. I was afraid Mohammed Nabi was going to call out the gunner. He didn't. All he did was come ahead like a man the world had caved in on. I thought of the time I was dragged over the rocks by his orders. I thought of the tied dick and the water that was about to be forced into me until my bladder ruptured. Come on, Mohammed Nabi, old pal! Just get a little closer and you won't have to worry any more about regional command.

When he was close enough, I opened fire.

SIX

The first burst killed four of them. Mohammed Nabi got it first and he did a little dance before he fell down dead. The last two tried to make it to cover. One of them dived for the brush like a swimmer going into a pool. I killed him on the wing and he went head over heels before he hit the ground. One was left and he was in cover and returning my fire. But he was rattled and not making the best use of his weapon.

Bullets tore bark from the tree behind me. The bullets kept coming, but he was still firing too high. There couldn't be many rounds left in his clip, but he wasn't using a semi-auto, so there was no way to tell how many. Another burst came, then stopped abruptly, and then I swung the light gun and raked his position with fire, running close to the end of the belt before I stopped firing. At first there wasn't a sound, then a strangled, sobbing noise came from the brush. I didn't move and I didn't fire. He might be crawling up on me, but I didn't think so. He wasn't a well trained soldier and he hadn't done anything right so far. It was a bit late for tricks.

I waited, and one by one, the birds came back. That was all the sign I needed, and I picked up the knife and went down the slope to make sure he was dead. The birds flew from one branch to another, but they didn't fly away. They were used to me by now; I had been there half the day.

I found the last Moro in the brush, lying on his side, the AK-47 still in his hands. Bullets had ripped into his chest and throat. I pried the rifle from his dead hands and took it back to where Mohammed Nabi and the others were. It never rains but it pours: now I had more top-notch weapons than I could carry. They would have to be checked out before I picked one to take away from there.

Mohammed Nabi had gone off with the diary in a canvas bag slung over his shoulder. There were two holes in the diary, a small stain of blood on the back cover. I dug out the bullets, but the only damage they had done was to the last ten months of Sanders' narrative. Nothing that mattered. I found the twenty thousand dollars. It was mine now, and I would have kept it even if Mrs. Sanders wasn't dead.

I put General Sanders' .45 in my belt, sat down, drank tepid water from Mohammed Nabi's canteen, and thought about what I was going to do. I could only guess where I was. Somewhere in central Mindanao, on the side of a mountain surrounded by even higher mountains.

I had to go with the idea that Mohammed Nabi had wiped out the government troops, losing two thirds of his force in the long firefight. If they had driven him off, they would be coming after him by now. Most likely they would. I turned my head to catch sounds on the wind, but heard nothing.

None of the dead men had been carrying the radio, which meant it had been lost during the fight. The government troops might be dead, but I knew a party from regional command would be coming after me once they failed to raise Mohammed Nabi on the radio. They might be on their way now, coming fast across the mountains. We had been traveling northeast; for now all I could do was go the other way and try to reach the coast and leave the islands by boat. I had enough money to bribe my way around the world, but the trouble with bribery is that usually they want to take all your money once they've taken part of it. The money I'd taken from Mohammed Nabi's body was a bonus I was ready to give up, but I didn't want to give up my life, which is how it works in most of these deals. They take you out to sea and then they throw you overboard to play with the sharks.

The people who murdered Mrs. Sanders would have their own interest in me; the Moros were a more pressing problem, because they were closer. They might be in Mindanao by now, but they had no tight fix on me yet. I figured some of them would trace me from Evangelista to the bombed-out car; others would watch the ports and fishing villages when I didn't show up at the Zamboanga airport. That was how I saw it. I might be way off the mark, but all I had to work with was what seemed probable.

I wasn't hungry yet, but I was going to be: from here on in, even if I saw something to eat, I couldn't shoot it, and even if I shot it, I couldn't make a fire to cook it. There was no game in these mountains anyway, none that I could see. Mohammed Nabi and his Moros lived from one meal to the next, and their hard-times diet consisted of rice and chicken and fruit extorted from peasants or "donated" by them. They seldom had enough to eat, but they made do with what they had. I wasn't going to be so lucky. I had nothing.

I searched the bodies for a map, a compass, anything that would help me get to the coast. Nothing like that. These guys hadn't needed maps or compasses. All I turned up was a few photographs of wives, children, sweethearts. A few pesos, more centavos than pesos. A Philippine peso is worth about $7.50; a hundred centavos make up a peso, so you can see how poor they were. One guy had been carrying a dirty postcard in his hip pocket. It showed a girl and a pony and had been given to the world by the Happy Times publishing company of Manila. I found an old Barlow knife and put it in my pants pocket.

Mohammed Nabi, as befitted a leader, had been carrying the newest AK-47 in the outfit. But newest doesn't have to mean best kept, and I checked it out before I decided it was okay. Extra clips were no problem; I had more ammunition than I could carry. The clip in place was loaded to capacity, so I figured two back-up clips would be enough. It was time to say goodbye to my friends.

Two main rivers flow through Mindanao: Rio

Grande de Mindanao and the Agustan. I knew that from the map I no longer had. If I could find the Agustan, then maybe I could make my way to the south coast without being spotted by whoever was after me. I didn't know and I might never know if they saw me before I saw them.

I was able to fill two canteens from all the canteens I piled up. A nice collection of slops, but it would have to do until I found water fit to drink. Then after one check I headed west along the side of the mountain, scouting the valley below with binoculars when there was a break in the trees. Like the other villages, there had been rice paddies there before the guerrilla war started. Now it was just swampland, black ooze covered by a carpet of dark green, dangerous in the places where it was deep.

The Moros had been following an ancient mountain trail, but now there were no trails of any kind, and I had to use the machete all the time to make any progress. I had been sweating when I started out. Now, less than an hour later, my feet were squelching in my own sweat; I spattered sweat as I moved. It rained and I felt better for a while. That didn't last. I was losing water as fast as I could take it in. There was nothing to do but sit down and drink again.

Two miles from where I started, I sat down and rested. I took the diary out of Mohammed Nabi's canvas bag and looked at it. It was getting damp and soon it would be mildewed. After that it would begin to rot. Six or seven hundred pages of stiff paper bound in leather. A heavy piece of work. A lot of dead weight to be carrying—to where? The woman who hired me to find it was dead, so there was no rightful owner that I could see. I didn't see that I owed anything to anybody. A true-blue patriot would have struggled over hill and dale to deliver it to the "proper authorities," and I might just do that if I came across an army intelligence booth on the side of the mountain, but I wasn't going to get worked up about it. I thought of the old joke about the cannibal with indigestion: "I like missionary, but missionary don't like me." That was how I felt about intelligence agencies. They got paid to do their job, so let them do it without any help from me.

I wanted to throw the damn thing away. Instead, I put it back in the bag, picked up the machete and started out again. Later I might chuck it into the brush, where it would disintegrate in no time, but for now I was going to hang onto it. A lot of people had died because of it, but that wasn't it. And it wasn't because I figured to sell it for big money. My principal reason, not too well thought out, was that I had taken one hell of a beating to get it; I felt the God damned thing belonged to *me.*

It got dark before I hacked my way through another mile of brush, and there was nothing to do but sleep where I was and start again at first light. There was no twilight; darkness fell like a blanket. In the Philippines, it cools off at night, but it doesn't get cold. Where I was, in the rain forest, it gets noisy; everything that can twitter and grunt and hoot comes out to sound off. There was nothing to eat, but my belly hadn't started growling yet, so that was all right. I drank tepid water, put my back against a tree and fell asleep with an AK-47 across my knees.

By noon the next day I went down into the

valley and the going got easier. The place where I had killed the Moros was about five miles behind, and I thought I was safe enough. I made my way along the edge of the abandoned rice paddies, now gone back to swamp, stopping to rest every two hours. My water was going fast. I drank what I thought I needed; that "one mouthful of water" stuff works in the movies but not in real life. I hoped I was heading for the Agustan river, or any river. If not, I would have to drink swamp water, stagnant and stinking, and hope it wouldn't bring on a fever that would kill me.

That night I climbed up from the valley to sleep under the trees, and the mosquitos from the swamp bit me bloody by morning. They bit through my shirt, and through the mud I had smeared on my face and neck and hands, but I slept in spite of everything. I woke up hungry as well as dirty. The sun was up strong. I had slept late, exhausted by all that machete swinging. I drained what was left in the second canteen and started down into the swampy valley.

There was a brief downpour along about ten o'clock and I caught some of the rain in my hat. I drank that and kept going. The valley ran for miles; one part of it looked like any other. Men had planted and harvested rice here for hundreds, maybe thousands of years, but now the wilderness was taking the land back. That's how it is in the tropics: leave something untended for a few years and it will disappear. First the outlines will go, then the thing itself.

The valley came to an end by late afternoon, and I climbed up out of it. Then I had to cross some low hills covered with sun-withered grass

95

and bare of brush and trees. Here I made the best time of all, but there wasn't a sign of water. I came across the bleached skeleton of a carabao, one of the water buffalo used by the farmers to plow rice fields. It looked as if it had been there for years, but I changed my mind when I saw the bullet holes in the skull. The farmers suffered, no matter who was winning the war.

There was still some light left when I came to the top of a long grassy slope and saw the river in the distance. I wasn't dying of thirst, but it doesn't take long to go from being thirsty to falling down from lack of water. It was a big wide river and the sinking sun glinted on the water. If it had been closer I might have hurried, but it was miles away, and so I kept my pace steady. Before I started down the other side of the hill I scouted the river with the binoculars and didn't see anything. The river might be the Agustan and at that point it flowed from north to south. Right then I didn't much care where it emptied into the sea. I just wanted a drink of water.

Between the hills and the river was rolling grassy country, with no hills or swamps to cross. It was good and dark before I was halfway across, but I kept going, thinking of nothing but cool, clean water. I made it there in less than an hour and forced myself to stop and listen before I left my weapons and the diary on a little sandy beach and threw myself face down in the shallows and drank until I was gasping. The moon came out and I could see the river flowing dark and fast. There were no lights anywhere and no sounds except the tiny waves the fast flowing water made on the beach.

I edged into deep water with my clothes on, watching for a drop that might take me out into the current. But the sand remained firm and flat, and I took off my clothes and washed them, scrubbing at the swamp mud with handfuls of river sand. Then I threw the wet clothes on the beach and washed myself, enjoying the rasp of sand against my bug-bitten skin. I stayed in the cool water for a long time.

Later I rinsed the canteens and refilled them after I spread out my clothes to dry. There was a warm night wind, but it felt like a mountain breeze after the furnace heat of the day. My belly was starting to growl and I filled it with good clean water and I felt all right after that. I let my clothes dry a little before I put them on and lay down in the sand and slept. It was the best sleep I'd had since I ran into Mohammed Nabi and his Moros.

No boats were on the river when I woke up at first light. No signs of human life on my side of the river, or on the far shore. On the other side of the river there were hills that turned into mountains after a few miles. Fog rolled on the surface of the water, but you could see over it. The river was deep, the current was fast and smooth. If I had a boat, I thought : . .

I had water for breakfast. Then I rinsed the canteens and filled them again before I started downstream. Most of the time I could stay by the edge of the river, but now and then I came to marshy places and had to climb up and walk on the high ground. The sun came up strong and I sweated, but I felt all right even with the growling in my belly and the fatigue that comes when you're sweated too much and don't have salt tablets to make up for the loss of salt.

A few hours later, I came to a burned village by the side of the river. It was more a scatter of huts than a real village, but there had been life there once. The poles that had supported the burned landing stuck up out of the water. I poked through the ruins of the village, thinking maybe I'd find a can of food. Big, timid rats resembling South American agoutis ran away from me. There were piles of empty cans in a trash pit, but no food. I saw some bleached skulls in the rubble.

It rained where I was; downriver the sun was shining. I drank as much water as I could, because I might be forced to leave the river at any time, and it's better to have water in you than in your canteen. Every few miles I dipped myself in the river, making the most of all that water.

I followed the river into a wide, flat valley with mountains that came down close to the edge of the water. At that time of day the valley was in shadow. Out of the sun it was a few degrees cooler; the brush that grew along the riverbank made it hard to get through; in the reeds I saw the same big rats I'd seen back in the village. I wasn't starving yet, but I was getting there, because I found myself wondering how river rat tasted when eaten raw.

After the valley came to an end, there was a wide bend in the river and the mountains, no longer crowding in, flattened out a bit. Along the mountain slopes were miles of hardwoods, not so much brush. You don't find much brush where the hardwoods grow. I got rid of my sweat by lying in the shallows and letting the water flow over me, then I went up the slope under trees and dug around with the knife, looking for roots—anything—that might fill my belly. After a lot of digging, I found a cluster of yellowish bulbs that looked and tasted like wild onions.

I chewed half a bulb and swallowed it and waited for the results. Like they say, if it looks like a duck, walks and squawks like a duck, then it probably is a duck. These, I decided, were wild onions, so I ate the rest of the bunch. I drank water to kill the bitter taste. Before I moved on, I dug up more onions for later. I was all set to go into partnership with some guy who owned a steak.

Like I said, the hardwoods ran for miles on both sides of the river. Millions of dollars of valuable timber; no wonder Marcos didn't want to give up Mindanao to the Moros. My thoughts had moved on to something besides hardwoods when I heard the whine of an electric saw far downriver. The sound came to me as soon as I followed the river round a bend and it straightened out again. The sound, coming up the flat surface of the river, was unmistakable. Somebody was operating a sawmill in Moro country, with a guerrilla war going on. At first I thought it had to be Moros, but when I got closer and used the binoculars, I saw an Australian flag flapping from a tall flagpole. I had to get down into the water before I was able to see anything else. I saw buildings close to the water, a sturdy dock supported by piles, and while I watched, a tall white man in shorts and bush hat got into a metal boat with an outboard motor and went across to the other side of the river. He pulled the boat up on the sand and went up into the trees. I didn't get any of it and I didn't care; the Australians like their steaks and so do I.

The whine of the saw killed all other sound as I got closer. That was why I didn't hear the guard come up behind me. I whirled when the muzzle of his rifle touched my spine, but he backed off just as fast and held the rifle steady on my belly. He was about thirty, short and thin, with a sweat-stained bush hat pulled down over his eyes. His bony face was badly sunburned; dead skin was peeling from his nose, and his bright blue eyes regarded me with deep suspicion. He said something I couldn't hear, but I knew he was telling me to put my hands up. His rifle was a sporting piece, a five-shot Remington, not new but well looked after. I raised my hands and he sort of pointed with the rifle without moving it away from me. Then he nodded his head in the direction of the camp and I walked on in front of him. He didn't try to take my weapons.

We were very close when the saw stopped and the man behind me fired off one shot, then chambered a fresh round. The saw remained quiet, but there was shouting beyond the trees, and in seconds there were men with rifles out on the docks, looking upriver, shading their eyes against the sun.

"I'm an American," I said to the man with the rife. "The Moros captured me. I got away."

The Australian grunted. "Don't tell me, mate. Tell the boss."

Steps went up to the dock and when I was up there, they took my weapons and the canvas bag while the first guy kept me covered with the rifle. I was able to get a good look at the camp: two prefabricated buildings bolted together, a sawmill made of native wood. Huge piles of hardwood covered with tarpaulins. About half a mile of forest had been cleared along the river, which meant they had been there for some time. I counted fifteen of them; the guy on the other side of the river made sixteen. He was coming back across the river, the roaring outboard motor fighting the current.

The one in charge was a grizzled, red faced man in his late forties. He wore shorts, canvas shoes, a bush hat like the others. A long-stemmed briar pipe stuck out from between his tobacco-stained teeth, and he wasn't glad to see me.

"Now then," he said, in a pronounced Australian accent. "What are you supposed to be? Che Guevara or something? Or did you go out for a stroll and take a wrong turn? You're a bit off course, wouldn't you say?"

The other Aussies grinned at the boss man's sarcasm. He was a tough looking bird, but not especially mean. Two more Australians with sporting rifles came down from the trees to the dock. They must have been far out when the shot was fired. "Go back to your bloody posts," the boss man said wearily. "Che Guevara here may have brought a few friends along for company."

Well, I *was* wearing Cuban Army fatigues, I *was* carrying an AK-47. "I can explain the Cuban clothes," I said, and then I told him the rest of it, leaving out the diary. I said I was an American tourist and had been captured by the Moros about twenty miles from a village called Evangelista. They had taken me far into the mountains, but I stole an AK-47 and escaped.

"I followed the river down to here," I said.

"Why the Cuban gear?" the Australian asked.

"My clothes got wrecked and they gave me this to wear."

The Australian had been riffling through the money. "Very considerate of them," he said dryly. "A surprise to me. The Moros aren't known for their good deeds. They give you all this lolly so the pockets of your new suit wouldn't feel empty? My old dad always gave me a dollar when he bought me a new suit."

"The money belongs to me," I said. "And what I've told you is all true."

"Yes, of course it is," the Australian said. "So anyway, there you were in Moro country, minding your own business, with twenty thousand dollars in your pocket. You're not one for American Express, are you?"

"I always carry a lot of money," I said.

"You didn't plan to give it to the Moros?"

"Why would I want to do that? I told you I'm an American tourist. The Moros gave me the clothes, the weapons are Moro weapons."

"By way of Red China. Where are *you* by way of, chum?"

"San Francisco and Manila."

"What's the matter with Luzon? Don't they

have any interesting sights up north?"

"I wanted to see Mindanao," I said. "Look, I'm fucking hungry. You got anything to eat. I can answer questions and eat at the same time."

The boss man turned to the others and told them to go back to work. "Yank," he said to me, "you can eat till you're stuffed, but you'll have to come up with a better yarn than the one you've been telling me. This way to the dining room."

He led the way to one of the prefabs. It was divided into two sections. One end was a bunk-house, the other was where the crew ate. That section had a long folding table and chairs, a bar and a kitchen. The cook, who'd been on the dock, came in with us and waited to hear what I wanted to eat.

I settled for steak and eggs and coffee. The boss man sat across the table from me. "My name is Fitzgerald," he said. "You say yours is Rainey."

"It's my real name."

"Sure. It says so on your passport. You want a beer?"

He went to the makeshift bar and got two bottles of Swan lager from a cooler. "Whatever your real name is, Rainey will do for now. But we must get to the truth of it, old son. We're in a dicey situation here and I won't have you mucking us up. Now drink your beer and we'll have another go at it when you're feeling more candid."

The beer was ice cold and I drained the bottle in two long swallows. Fitzgerald's beer was gone and he got two more; in the kitchen the steak was sizzling. Big fans were booming in the windows and the forced air felt good on my skin. Fitzgerald waited until I finished the second bottle before he started in again.

"It would save a lot of time if you gave me the straight of it," he said. "It just won't do, that story of yours. Listen to what I tell you so you'll understand. You're wondering what a bunch of Australians are doing on the edge of Moro country. That's right, you made it that far. We had a small operation going here before the war hotted up. My company has a contract with the government, which means we have a contract with the Marcos family. The Marcos clan *is* the government. We thought we'd have to clear out when the Moros really went on the warpath. But we hung on, most of us, and little by little we worked out an arrangement with the Moros, or rather, the head office in Melbourne did. It was worked out with the Chinese. Australia is an Asian country, after all, or I should say it's a country in Asia. Like it or not, that's where we're stuck. These days we have a heavy trade with the Chinese and the Japanese, and not only that, we've been letting Asians come in as landed immigrants. That's done more than anything else to get rid of the ill will that's always attended our immigration policies. We used to be lily white, but that's a thing of the past, and a bloody good thing too. So Peking told the Moros to let us alone. They didn't like it, but they need the Chinese for weapons, money, supplies."

The cook brought in the steak-and-eggs and coffee. I salted and peppered the steak and started eating. I wanted to eat the steak with both hands, but I had company, so I used a knife and fork. Fitzgerald got two more beers.

"We've never had any Americans working for us," Fitzgerald went on. "And that's not because the company has anything against Yanks, but it's hard to do business in certain parts of Asia if you have Americans on the payroll. Americans aren't popular, lad, but I expect you know that. Even before Vietnam they weren't popular, and it's been far worse since then. Every time an Asian sees an American civilian attached to a company he thinks that company is controlled by the CIA. Ridiculous, of course, but those are the facts of life over here. Officially, then, we—my company—has absolutely no American connection. Now, unfortunately, we have one, and you're it."

"I'll be gone as soon as I eat this steak," I said. "You think you can give me some supplies?"

Fitzgerald knocked the ash out of his pipe and tamped in fresh tobacco. He thumbed an old Zippo and lit up, taking short puffs until he got it going right. I was just about done with the steak and the cook brought in most of a cold apple pie.

"Supplies are no problem," Fitzgerald said. *"You're* the problem and that yarn you've been spinning is an even bigger problem. Look at it from where I sit. You turn up here looking for all the world like a Cuban mercenary. You look the part right down to the hairy face and the AK-47. You've been in Moro country, a place where no tourist in his right mind would go, a place where white foreigners invariably end up as crow bait. So what do I think? Am forced to

105

think? I have to think you're an American mercenary working for the Moros. You got separated from your unit, perhaps in an ambush, or your Moro employers got nasty for some reason and you decided to make a run for it. The money, all that money? That's a bit of a puzzler, but how about this for a solution. You were sent to deliver a large amount of money to the Moros, much more than twenty thousand, and you decided to hold out the twenty thousand for yourself. That's been done, everything's been done. You ran into trouble when the Moros found out about it. But you managed to run, don't ask me how. Now would that be close to the truth?"

"No," I said. "Thanks for the steak. I'll be seeing you."

"Now I'm disappointed," Fitzgerald said. "I just hate it when I don't know what's going on. Usually I prefer to mind my own business, which is cutting up trees to send back to Australia, but this is altogether different. The point is, my camp may be under observation at this very moment. The lot of us may get shot before this is over and it would be nice if I knew what I was dying for. Why don't you make a clear breast of it, chum?"

"I told you what I told you. I'm sorry if you don't believe it."

"You mean 'swallow' not 'believe,' " Fitzgerald said mildy. "Swallow as in swallow lies. I'm as sorry as you are. Sorry I can't extend our fabled Australian hospitality without all these questions. But we live in dangerous times and suspicion of our fellow man is the name of the game. The thing of it is, I wouldn't take you for a tourist if you waltzed in here wearing a Hawaiian shirt and a porkpie hat with 'Kiss Me, I'm Irish' lettered on it. You *are* Irish, aren't you?"

"More or less."

"So am I. There, you see, we have something in common." Fitzgerald hummed a few bars of *Did Your Mother Come from Ireland?* "Nice old tune, that. Now as one Irishman to another, won't you tell me what you're doing here? You've eaten a nice steak and drunk some of our precious beer and I think it only fair that you give a better explanation than the one you've given. This climate is bad for my liver and I have been known to get annoyed when my patience is tried too far. Get the message?"

"It was a mistake to come here," I said.

"Yes, it was. Certainly it was if all you had to say was hello and goodbye. Nothing in this country is ever that simple."

"It can be. Forget you ever saw me. There's nothing to tie us together. You gave food to a man armed with an automatic rifle. Who wouldn't?"

"We wouldn't if we didn't want to," Fitzgerald said. "We don't have automatic rifles, but we do have rifles. We could have shot you any time. Some of my boys served with your people in Vietnam. You would have discovered that soon enough if you'd tried any rough stuff."

"I didn't come here looking for trouble."

"Of course you didn't. You came here half-starved with a silly yarn about being a lost tourist. Do you in your right mind expect any sensible man to believe that? Let me tell you something before you decide to spin some new

107

story you might think has a chance of getting past the goal-keeper. I've been bossing rough men for a great many years. I've had to tangle with even rougher men to keep them out of trouble, get them out of jail in five countries. I know when they're lying and when they're not. In short, I know men. Rough men, hard men, men like you. Come to think of it, I'm a pretty rough chap myself. Now would you like to try again?"

"I don't want to try anything, Fitzgerald. You've heard my story and you'll have to take it as it is. Or if you don't like that, why don't you make up your own story? It will do just as well. I thank you for the steak and the beer, but now I have to be going if you don't mind."

"Oh, but I do mind," Fitzgerald said.

SEVEN

I stood up to see what he would do. "You have no legal right to keep me here," I said, knowing it wasn't going to do any good. But I wanted to know how far he'd go with it.

"There's no law west of the Pecos," Fitzgerald said calmly. "You may have run away from the Moros, but you won't run away from me. Go out that door without my comforting presence and you'll be shot. Is that clear? I hope it is, because I'm not one for dramatics, and I don't mind telling you that killing you would get rid of the problem in the best possible way. But we won't kill you and you know it. What we will do, old son, is kick the shit out of you till you tell the truth. However, right now we're just having a nice chat, so sit down and eat your apple pie before it gets warm."

I sat down and started on a big wedge of pie. My story stank and sooner or later I'd have to tell the truth.

"That's better," Fitzgerald said, placing his

work-scarred hand on the diary, which lay on the table beside me. "Now I've said what I think you might be. That was for the sake of argument. But it's something else, isn't it? This book, for instance. You'll notice I haven't looked through it, because that wouldn't be polite, even under these circumstances. But I'll read your book and beat you up if there's no other way. Now why don't you make a general confession, as we R.C.'s say, and you'll feel so much better for having done it. I promise not to give you more than three Our Fathers and Three Hail Marys as your penance."

He was a funny guy in a sour sort of way, and I knew I wasn't going to get away with any more bullshit. I told him the whole story from start to finish, leaving out nothing. In for a penny, in for a pound, as he might say himself.

"Good Lord," he said when I finished. "That sounds like a yarn right out of *Boy's Adventure* magazine."

"It's no yarn," I said.

"Oh no, I didn't mean that," Fitzgerald said. "It's just that it's so bloody wild. You will admit it sounds pretty hairy. 'How I was saved by a snake in the Darkest Philippines' and all that— not that there aren't plenty of the buggers crawling about these woods. All I can say is, does your mother know what you do for a living, Rainey?"

"It has its moments," I said.

"Yes, I'm sure it does, but I think I'll stay with the business I'm in. But think of it! A bunch of fellas breaking their balls to get their hands on a forty-year-old diary. Most of the geezers named in it are dead, the rest of them tottering

110

on the edge of the grave. Mind if I ask what you intend to do with it?"

"I haven't made up my mind," I said.

"Then why not chuck it away?" Fitzgerald said. "It's all such ancient history, why get yourself bumped off by hanging onto it? I don't know how these things are done, but *you* must. Let it be known that you've destroyed the flipping diary and perhaps they'll write it off as old business."

"I'd do that if I thought it would work. The trouble is, they won't believe it. They'd just think I'd hidden it, to be picked up later when it was safe. As long as I have it, I have something to bargain with. I'm sorry I barged into your set-up, Fitzgerald."

"Call me Fitz. Well, you didn't mean to barge in, did you? I don't want to seem inhospitable, but we've got to get you out of here chop-chop. You've done for a whole bunch of Moros and those blighters at regional command will be looking for you. They must be looking for you at this very minute. They'll want your head as much as they want the diary. If they find out we've been harboring you, then it's goodbye for the lot of us. Then there's the government secret police to think about. They'll be frightfully angry, as the British say, if I don't report having seen you. Yes, I'm afraid I'll have to report you, but our radio just happens to be on the fritz, so that will take some time."

I smiled at the droll Aussie. "Is the radio on the fritz?"

"It is now," Fitzgerald said. He called the cook out of the kitchen. "Tell Dawkins to maintain radio silence till further orders. Tell him to

111

listen to what comes in, but there's to be no outgoing stuff. Got it?"

"Got it," the cook said, glancing at me before he went out.

"This could mean me job," Fitzgerald said, "but you look like a decent bloke to me and I won't have the Moros making off with your head. Our three boats are downriver right now, but one is due back tomorrow. As soon as it's loaded, you can get down to Davao. That's on the south coast of the island and a right busy place. Lots of tourists, lots of ships coming and going from other countries, lots of everything, including the secret police. I often think Marcos must have more secret policemen than he has soldiers. Bad boys, the lot of them. Many's the poor bastard they've salvaged for no reason at all."

"Salvaged?"

"Some sort of Filipino irony, I expect. A man who's drifted into Communism has to be 'salvaged.' Saved from the error of his ways. In short, killed. Odd, how the most ruthless men seldom use the word 'kill.' Their victims are 'eliminated,' 'liquidated,' 'chilled,' and so on. But they're just as dead, aren't they? But I don't mean to depress you, old chum. I'm sure nothing like that will happen to you."

"You have Filipinos working on your boats?"

"Nary a one. Good Aussies all. Hire on natives and at least one of them is going to be a secret policeman. I have enough problems without some little sod sending back false reports. The sneaky swine feel they have to gild the lily to make themselves look good. You'll be safe enough on the boat even if some river

112

patrol decides to make a search. I'll fix you up with a company ID card before you leave. Just burn it or eat it before you reach Davao. You never heard of the McGregor Company and we never heard of you."

"Thanks for doing this, Fitz."

"Thanks for what? I don't know what you're talking about. Get it?"

"Got it," I said.

"Well then, I'll show you to your quarters," Fitzgerald said, getting up from the table. I stood up too, and he looked me over. "I think we can fix you up with some new clothes. Then I suggest you stay in your room and read something uplifting. There are any number of greasy *Playboys* floating about the camp."

My quarters was a room in Fitzgerald's house, a bare, clean room with a camp bed and nothing else but a reading lamp screwed to the wall. Fitzgerald switched on the window fan and said there was plenty of food and beer in the refrigerator. "Books in the living room if you find *Playboy* too much of a strain on the nerves. Books get mildewed in this sodding climate, but I'm sure you'll find something to read. Anything else you can think of?"

"Yeah," I said, grinning. "I know you guys favor shorts, but you think you can find me a pair of long pants?"

"What's wrong with short, mate? They're the only sensible gear for the tropics."

"I'd feel like an idiot in shorts, Fitz."

Fitzgerald rolled his eyes in mock exasperation. "Oh, you Yanks and the peculiar ideas you have! Nobody's going to laugh at you out here, you know. Nobody's going to snap your picture.

113

But very well, if it's long pants you want, then it's long pants you shall have."

At the door he turned and said, "Take it easy, Yank. You're tight as a piano wire. Loosen up and get some sleep."

I stripped to my under shorts and lay down on the bed, but sleep wasn't so easy to come by. Fitzgerald was right. I was bone tired; even so, I lay awake for a long time listening to the work sounds of the camp. Finally, I slept and there were shadows in the room when I was awakened by shouting in the compound. I had slept through the whine of the saw, but these sounds were different. Something was going on down there. I went to the window and saw Moros all over the place. There must have been thirty or forty of the bastards, all heavily armed and in a killing mood. Most of the shouting was being done by a skinny guy in a Cuban uniform. He had a wispy beard and wore a kind of flat red turban instead of a Castro cap. He had the Australians lined up and was shouting at Fitzgerald. I had no idea what language he was speaking, but Fitzgerald seemed to know it, because he talked and gestured and kept shaking his head in denial of what he was being charged with. The argument went on and the Moro got madder by the minute.

I stiffened when Fitzgerald pointed to the Australian flag and the Moro slapped him across the face. But there was nothing I could do except watch; even a machine-gun wouldn't have done me any good; there was just too many of them down there. Fitzgerald took the slap and kept his temper. After some more yelling at Fitzgerald, the Moro turned and yelled something to his men and cold sweat broke out on my face when they raised their automatic rifles and took aim at the Aussies—not that they needed to take aim at point-blank range. I waited for the rattle of the AK-47's, but it didn't come. Then, suddenly, the Moro leader began to laugh; they all began to laugh, pointing at the Aussies, really cracking up at the humor of it all. Then the leader said something else and a bunch of Moros ran into the bunkhouse and came out, dragging the beer cooler and all the food they could find. The Australians watched while the Moros knocked the heads off the beer bottles and drank by holding the bottles over their heads and letting the beer splash into their mouths. They say Muslims don't drink, but I guess these bastards were a long way from Mecca. They were down to the last bottle of cold beer, and were looking mad about it, when some guy who was poking around found six cases of beer in a shack and came running with a case in his arms, yelling the good news. They were just getting started on that when a Chinese and a Cuban came down the slope from the trees. The Chinese was young, but he had a stiff leg and walked with a cane. The Cuban, about the same age, walked close beside him as if to make sure he wouldn't keel over. A heartwarming display of Marxist cooperation.

They were close to the top of the slope when one of the Moros who hadn't seen them raised his automatic rifle and shot holes in the Australian flag. He fired off a whole clip before he blew away the flag and the rope and the top of the flagpole. He was loading a fresh clip when the lame Chinese spoke sharply in a high sing-song voice. The Moro leader, drunk on beer, turned to look at him. He shouted at the Chinese and the Chinese shouted back, making many gestures. For a moment, I thought the Moro was going to open fire on the two men, then his nerve gave and he lowered his weapon, looking so sullen that I wasn't sure that he wouldn't change his mind and drop the Chinese and the Cuban in a hail of bullets.

Ignoring him, the Chinese walked up to Fitzgerald and spoke so softly that I couldn't hear a word he was saying. He spoke at length and every time he paused, Fitzgerald shook his head and said something of his own. All that took a while, when the Chinese bowed, turned to the Moro and pointed to the river. The Moro scowled and the Chinese had to raise his voice to an even louder pitch before the Moro and his men went down to the boats they had come in. I watched while they hoisted sail and the boats glided swiftly away, propelled by wind and current. The Chinese and the Cuban were the last to leave, two commanders who preferred to direct operations from the rear.

Now it was just minutes to sundown and Fitzgerald walked over and looked up at the window. "You can come down now, Rainey. Come down and have a beer."

I went down. Fitzgerald was as calm as if nothing more alarming than a troop of boy scouts had passed through. "Pity about the flagpole," he said, "but we can always make a new one. I feel worse about the flag. Those sodding bastards, what did they have to shoot the flag for?" It was the first time I had seen him

116

show anger. Then he smiled and began to fill his pipe. "The bastards will be back, but not for days, that is if they don't run into a government patrol boat. If they do, they'll be blown out of the water and amen to that. Pray tell, what are you looking so serious about?"

I took the warm beer he handed me. "I've got to get the fuck away from here before I get you all killed."

"Not tonight, Rainey," Fitzgerald said between preliminary puffs on his pipe. "Some of the lads are a bit pissed off at you, but so would you be if you'd recently been looking down the barrel of an automatic rifle. Don't worry about it. They'll get over it as soon as they realize what heroes they are. But ain't I glad that Chinaman showed up when he did! We'd all have been dead before they got to the end of the beer. Actually, I'm not sorry it happened, now that I think about it. In a way, it makes our position here that much stronger. Let's just hope nothing happens to that lovely Chinaman. Cheer up, old son. Everything came out all right in the end. I suppose it comes of living a clean life."

"What time will the boat be here tomorrow?" I asked.

Fitzgerald shrugged. "I would say between nine o'clock and noon. We have a schedule but seldom get to keep it. Things get in the way. Heavy traffic on the lower river. Inspections by river patrols. Or a strong wind can be blowing the wrong way. Don't fret about the blood boat. It'll get here."

And it did, a few minutes after ten thirty. We'd eaten breakfast hours before and now we drank beer on the dock and watched the empty boat being loaded with a new cargo of hardwood. After the hardwood reached Davao, it would be loaded onto freighters bound for Australia.

"Here's your ID card," Fitzgerald said. "You take a lousy photograph, you know that? You're simply not photogenic. Notice how the card has been artfully aged in spite of being laminated? Those scratches on the plastic make it just right, don't you think? How's your Australian accent, by the way? Not that the river police will know the difference."

"Stone the crows," I said. "Fair dinkum. The Sydney sheilas are the prettiest gels in the world. Ned Kelly camped by a billabong."

Fitzgerald grinned. "Jolly good," he said. "Just don't try that on a strange Australian or he'll punch you in the nose. Here"—he took the .45 from his pants pocket—"you'll probably be needing this. I chucked the automatic rifle in the river, and a good thing too. If they'd found it . . . well, we won't dwell on that. Now listen to me, old son, what you do after this is your business, but if I were in your position I'd give serious thought to getting on board one of our freighters. They're company owned and don't take passengers—no exception to this rule—but a smart lad like yourself should be able to find a way around that. Find a good place to hide so they'll be far out at sea before they find you or you give yourself up. The captain won't be pleased to find he has a stowaway aboard, but if he's far enough out, he won't turn back to put you ashore. He may or may not lock you in the brig. That's up to him, but the grub won't be too bad and you'll be in Melbourne in no time. You'll face charges, of course, and may even have to spend a few months in jail. What does it matter? You'll be ordered to leave the country or face deportation. With twenty thousand in your pocket, you'll be only to happy to oblige. Happy ending to otherwise grim story."

"I'll think about it, Fitz."

"Think about it hard, old son. It may be the only way to get away from these islands." Fitzgerald finished his Swan lager and stood up. "They're about done with the loading. Time to be off. We run these things like oil tankers, in and out of port in the fastest possible time."

We went down to the boat, a long, wide steel vessel of shallow draft, and Fitzgerald held out his hand. "Take care of yourself, Rainey. You might send me a postcard some time."

"Thanks, Fitz," was all I said, then I went on board, the motors started up and the boat edged away from the dock. Fitzgerald was walking up the slope to the compound when I turned to look back.

The boat was called *MacGregor 27,* not much poetry in that, and it had a captain, a mate, six crewmen. It could have been operated with a smaller crew, but Australia is the most unionized country in the world and they do everything by the book. Later, on the river, I was to listen to hours of bickering over this and that union rule, the difference in pay scales in various parts of Australia, the best strike ever. One guy named Gootch was a regular sea lawyer and was forever going to the captain with complaints. Every time he scored a point,

119

he would grin like a monkey and do a little jig; he spent all his off-duty time reading books on labor law.

The captain, a Queenslander named Richardson, talked to me when he felt like it. He didn't like having me on board, but Fitzgerald bossed the entire operation, so the captain didn't go out of his way to be unpleasant. But he did tell me to keep out of the way, to do nothing that would interfere with the running of the boat.

I had to bunk in with the crew. Living quarters, bridge and galley were all astern. The captain and mate, a glum guy named Smithers, had tiny cabins to themselves; the rest of us were thrown together in a large space with camp beds screwed to the floor. A big short-wave radio, property of the company, was seldom turned off. It brought in Sydney and other Austrailian cities; native punk rock was the favorite of all but Gootch, who wanted to listen to serious discussion shows, but was always overruled.

Fitzgerald had told the captain all he needed to know about me. The crew knew I was an American and a friend of Fitzgerald's, but that's all they knew. What they didn't know made them curious. This turned to resentment when I didn't come across with any information about myself and why I was hitching a ride on their boat. I sat in on some of their interminable poker games, letting them win a few bucks, never enough to make me look like a patsy. They had fans going in the windows—no portholes on this boat—but it was hot on the river and there was always the sickly sweet smell of raw timber.

There wasn't that much to running the boat; the river was wide and deep, with no islands or rapids to make it hazardous. The only real hazard was the Moros, but there wasn't a sign of the flotilla that had gone downstream searching for me. The captain had seen them on the way up, had told Fitzgerald about it, had been assured that there was nothing to worry about. It didn't take him long to make the connection between the Moros and me, and when he did, he frowned whenever he saw me sitting out on deck. He would have liked it better if I had stayed out of sight. If he had ordered me off the deck, I would have obeyed without question, but since he didn't, I stayed where I was.

The miles of hardwood gave out and now the tangled rain forest grew right down to the edge of the water. Back of the rain forest were mountains, one higher than the other. We went through a long gorge where the cliffs on both sides shut out the sun. There, the current was very swift and the helmsman had his work cut out for him. Then we were back in blinding sunlight and the surface of the river was so smooth that the fast-moving boat seemed to be running in a river of oil.

It got dark and they cut back on the speed; even so, the boat moved along at a fair clip, its lights reflected in the dark water. A watch was posted forward to keep a lookout for obstructions, native boats or floating trees, anything that could get into the steering gear and sent the boat spinning all over the river. The boat had a steel hull, but there were rocks along the banks that could gash its sides and sink it if it went out of control.

Supper that night was steak and mashed potatoes swimming in gravy. Most of the men drank beer; Australians drink beer the way Southerners drink Royal Crown Cola. All this beer guzzling would never be allowed on an American boat, but I guess they had the suds written into their union contract. They drank a lot of beer; they never got drunk, not even tipsy.

The second day was much the same as the first. I asked the sea lawyer how far we'd come and he said it wasn't the duty of a crew member to enter into such calculations. "We'll be in Davao early in the morning," he said. "I trust this bit of knowledge will set your mind at rest." That was the way he talked.

During the night there was shouting and I got up to see what was going on. The captain, irritable in striped pajamas, shouted at the watch and the wtach shouted back, saying there were bodies and wreckage in the river. That woke up the captain and he yelled, "Stop engines" and went forward with the mate. The whole crew were turned out by now and all but the helmsman went forward to take a look. I followed along, knowing the captain would be too busy to get mad at me for mixing in.

The forward searchlight clicked on, lighting up the river in a sudden, blinding flash. Smithers, the mate, moved the light down the water. Bodies were rolling in the water, close to shore where the current wasn't so swift. One body hung over the keel of a capsized boat. There were bullet holes in the corpse and in the boat. The mast of another sunken boat stuck up out of the shallow water by the starboard bank. Bits of wood and rope and canvas floated downriver ahead of us. I saw the body of the Moro who didn't like to take orders from Chinamen.

The captain pointed to the dead Moro's red turban. "That's the fella we saw coming upriver. Looks like the patrol boats shot up their whole fleet. These days they carry rockets, all kinds of heavy stuff. Sweet Jesus Christ! Will you look what they did to those Moros!"

"Good for them," the mate said. "You ask me, the only good Moro is a dead Moro."

The captain hocked up phlegm and spat in the river. "Start engines," he said. "We'll proceed dead slow till we're clear of this shit. There must be more of it downriver. Relieve the watch and send him aft. You'd think he never saw a dead body before."

I tried to get out of there before the captain saw me, but he was too quick. "I suppose this takes a load off your mind, Mr. Rainey," he said.

I grunted something.

"Yes indeed," he said. "It certainly takes a load off *my* mind. I was afraid . . . but never mind that. We'll be docking in Davao in the morning. Goodnight, Mr. Rainey."

"Goodnight, Captain," I said.

I lay awake thinking of the dead men in the river. The captain was satisfied that all the Moros had been wiped out; I wasn't so sure. More than likely, the main force had been destroyed, but what about the Chinese and the Cuban? They hadn't gone downriver until the main force was already on its way. They hadn't been far behind—just far enough, maybe, to get ashore while the Moros were being slaughtered by rockets and heavy machine-guns. The

123

Chinese was crippled, but he had come a long way in an effort to find me, to find the diary. If he had survived, then he would keep on looking. Too many people were looking for me.

EIGHT

Early morning. The river had widened to become an estuary, and we were coming into the port of Davao, when we came abreast of a patrol boat that was moving downriver at slow speed. It looked like a PT-Boat from World War II, except that it was much smaller and was armed with rockets instead of torpedoes. It had been badly shot up: I knew the engines had been damaged by the sound they made. Wounded men, maybe some dead men, lay on the deck; there was a lot of bullet holes, a lot of blood turning black in the sun. Then I saw the Cuban handcuffed to the railing. His cap was gone and his face was covered with blood and he hung over the rail with only the handcuffs to keep him from falling into the water. We moved on and river traffic get between us and the shot-up boat.

"That fella looked like a Cuban," the captain said to the mate. "They must have captured him after they did for the Moros."

"Good luck to them," the mate said. "I hate

fucking Cubans. Why don't they stick to rhumba music like Desi Arnaz? Why do they have to go exporting revolution all the time?"

The captain spat in the oily waters of the harbor. "He'll be sorry he didn't stay in Cuba once the secret police get their dirty hands on him. Ah well, another day, another dollar. Let's get on with it, Mr. Smithers."

We edged in to the MacGregor dock and tied up. I said goodbye to the captain and he nodded, but didn't offer to shake hands. I think he was a tough, competent man in his way; sure as hell he was no Fitzgerald.

There were uniformed policemen on the dock. They looked me over with brief professional interest as I went ashore and started up into the town. A busy town, Davao, just as Fitzgerald has described it. Freighters were tied up all along the docks; others, at anchor, were spotted in various parts of the harbor. Far out, too big to come in, a cruise ship stood up white and tall against the bright morning sky. The smell of the sea was everywhere.

I had no idea where I was going, but that was all right. First I would take a look at the town, then take it from there. There was a wide street called Rizal Street with a lot of bars and tourist shops on both sides. I went into a bar that called itself GI Joe's, pushed my way through the crowd of early morning drinkers, and ordered a bottle of San Miguel, the only beer they make in the Philippines and very good beer it is, too.

The guy who owned or managed the place stood behind the bar, but didn't help with the drinks. He wore a loud print shirt, had a thinning blond crewcut, and looked a little like Red Buttons. Old regular army was stamped all over him, from the way he talked to the way he stood. He had a line of snappy chatter for everybody in sight, and I decided he wasn't unaware of his resemblance to the redheaded comedian. "So the patient said to the psychiatrist: 'Doctor, do you think sex is dirty?' and the psychiatrist answers back, 'It is if you do it right.' "

That really knocked them out and the man in the print shirt got off five more swifties before I finished the first beer and ordered another. While I was drinking it, another American, a heavyset guy with a red face and a rumpled white suit, came in and ordered a rum and Coke.

"Hey Joe, whaddaya know?" he said to the man in the print shirt.

"I was sick in bed with the nurse, but I'm all right now," Joe said. "How's by you, Eddie?"

"Still hanging in there, Joe," Eddie said. "Ya can't let the bastards grind ya down."

Even today, you can still find places like GI Joe's in the United States, but you have to look hard. In former outposts of empire—Panama, the Philippines—those bars and the men who drink in them, tell jokes in them, are frozen in time, say, July 4th, 1939. That was a good year for Americans: the Depression was almost over and America, very sure of itself, stood in splendid isolation from the crazy Europeans rushing toward war. Joe and Eddie were about that vintage; in late middle age but still frisky, they must have been very young when Pearl Harbor came.

I thought of all this because a faded sign over

the bar said REMEMBER PEARL HARBOR; other patriotic slogans kept it company. It was that kind of place. GI Joe didn't look like any kind of crook, just an old retired top sergeant who'd been in the islands too long to even think about going "home." But a crook or a fixer was what I wanted and I wasn't going to find him here. I drank my beer and went out.

I didn't have all that much time to make my move. The Moros had their agents in Davao, all the Mindanao ports; the secret police were as thick as fleas in the same places. I could only guess at the identity of the man, or men, who had murdered Mrs. Sanders. It wasn't the Moros, so I had a choice between the secret police or thugs hired by one or more of the people named in the diary. There was even the possibility that people in the Manila underworld had got word of the diary and saw it as a way to make millions in blackmail.

I wondered how the Cuban was getting along with the secret police. It would be a new experience, that was for sure. The white-suited Gestapo would want to know what he was doing so far downriver in company with a large force of Moro guerrillas. He was probably a tough guy and would try to stall them with all the techniques he had learned in survival school. None of it would work; he'd talk in the end and when he did, the secret police would know I was on the loose and probably heading for Davao. How much time I had depended on how tough the Cuban was. Be tough, *amigo,* I thought. Show those runty Filipinos what a *macho* man you are.

I rented a room close to the waterfront; from

there I could see the MacGregor docks. The boat I'd been on was tied up behind the two other timber boats. Nothing had been unloaded; they were waiting for a MacGregor cargo ship to arrive from Australia. Three of the timber boats made a full cargo for a single cargo ship. The one they were waiting for was due in that afternoon. It was early afternoon now, but it hadn't arrived. I wasn't sure I wanted to play stowaway, but maybe it was better than nothing.

Outside my window there was a little balcony and I sat there under a sun umbrella and looked at the other boats with binoculars. There were freighters from all over the world. Getting on board one of those was a possibility; the trouble with freighters was that even the captain himself didn't always know where his next port of call might be. Freighters changed by cabled or radioed instructions from the home office. I didn't want to sneak on board in Davao and end up in Zamboanga, or Manila, or any of a hundred ports between Luzon and Mindanao.

I moved the binoculars to the cruise ship riding at anchor outside the entrance to the harbor. Another possibility. Cruise ships sailed like clockwork; it took some man-made or natural disaster to throw them off their schedules. I had a passport, but that wouldn't get me on board. What I needed was one of those landing passes issued by the purser. Passengers could take their passports ashore, if that was what they wanted to do, but it was discouraged by the cruise ship companies, who explained that anyone carrying a valid passport became a target for thieves. Most countries honored the landing passes provided the tourists who had them didn't remain ashore more than twenty-four hours. The cruise ship flew the Dutch flag and I wondered what kind of food they served in the brig.

I was still on the balcony when three jeep-loads of uniformed police drove down to the docks and swarmed all over the MacGregor boats. A black Mercedes came last and four men in civilian clothes got out and held a brief consultation before going on board *MacGregor 27*. It looked like the Cuban had talked and now the secret police were following through on his information. The uniformed police searched the boats, then came ashore and stood on the dock, talking and smoking, waiting for instructions from the guys who came in the Mercedes. Through the glasses I could see the four secret policemen interrogating the captain. A few times they poked him in the chest, but that was as rough as they got. They came ashore at last and one of them spoke to the ranking uniformed cop. The cop saluted and the Mercedes and one Jeep drove away. After that, the cops who were left watched the three timber boats as if they expected them to sprout wings and fly away.

The MacGregor cargo ship came into the harbor and was alongside by four o'clock. Fili-pino dockers were waiting to load the hard-wood, but the officer in charge of the uniformed police detail came stomping down the dock and waved them back. Through the binoculars I could see the cords standing out on his neck, the way his eyes bulged with mindless rage.

Put an Asian in a police uniform and he becomes an instant bully, browbeating the poor, kissing the asses of those in authority. When his tantrum petered out, he talked into a walkie-talkie, then stood around with his chest puffed out until the Mercedes showed up again. The same four secret policemen got out and boarded the cargo ship by crossing the walkway that had been set up between *MacGregory 27* and the cargo ship, which was named *MacGregor 5.* The captain came down from the bridge and there was a lengthy consultation on the forward deck. It came to an end, and they left the boat.

The Filipinos started the loading of the cargo ship, while the uniformed police sat on crates, talking and smoking. One of them went to a dockside bar and came back with a bag of beer; the Philippine constabulary aren't too well disciplined. As soon as the ban on loading was lifted, the crew of the cargo ship went up into the town. The police looked after them, then lost interest because there was no easy way to shake them down for money.

It looked like *MacGregor 5* was a bust as a getaway boat. I couldn't understand why they hadn't staked out the freighters that lined the dock. But maybe they were watching and I couldn't see them. It could be part of a plan; the secret police were vicious, crooked bastards, but I was sure they knew their job.

A big launch was coming in from the cruise ship; another was going out. Both launches were filled with tourists in bright clothes. They lined the rail, holding onto it, pointing at this and that. There were a lot of cameras going. A tall officer in whites was pointing out the sights. I watched them come ashore.

I went to Rizal Street and bought some tourist clothes in a store owned by a Chinese. Light blue slacks, yellow shirt, white canvas shoes, an African hunter's hat with a leopard-skin band. The same store sold me aviator sunglasses and an Instamatic camera with carrying case and strap. I put on the new clothes in a curtained booth. The Chinese bundled up my old stuff, and I went out into the glare and noise.

Down the street, a bunch of pentecostals in shabby white uniforms were doing an impersonation of the Salvation Army, knocking out "Rock of Ages" with piano accordian, trombone and tambourine. They had to fight hard to make themselves heard above the god-awful racket of the ghetto blasters, the big suitcase radios carried by just about every kid on the street. Beside the band was a canvas bin for old clothes. I put my bundle in the bin and ten dollars in the collection bucket.

When I got to the end of Rizal Street, the Dutch officer was already there with his mob of tourists, moving them along like sheep, making sure none of the blue-haired ladies was grabbed and sold into white slavery. He carried a miniature bullhorn and he knew how to use it; his voice came out of it in soothing though amplified tones. The Dutch and the Swedes speak the best English in Europe, and this handsome Dutchman had just enough of an accent to make him interesting to the ladies. One of the ladies was saying to another lady, "It's just like *Love Boat,* isn't it?"

All the ladies had big bags. My bag was an Icelandic Airlines flight bag from the Chinese tourist trap. The Chinaman said it was a big seller with the tourists, because, see, it was a good joke and a real conversation starter to carry a bag from such a cold country in such a hot country. I got the joke and I bought the bag. I saw five bags like it after I left the shop. I had the diary in the bag.

I tagged along behind the Dutchman and his flock, and I'll bet I was the only one in the bunch with a .45 under his shirt. Now the Dutchman was promoting cold drinks and ice cream. "What do you think, guys?" He actually called them "guys." "There's a very nice place in the next block."

We all went in, me last, and sat on wire chairs while the waitresses, dressed like Swiss milkmaids, ran around taking orders. The air conditioning was turned to minus zero. There were other tourists there, but they didn't have the placid, shepherded look of those from the cruise ship. A few well-dressed touts were hanging around with the blessing of the management. I guess they split the take, but there wouldn't be any rough stuff or downright swindling.

There were photographic murals of the Alps; signs warned skiers of impending avalanches. Other signs on poles pointed the way to famous ski resorts, and the Filipino men behind the counter all wore embroidered shirts and Tyrolean hats. A jukebox was playing snow tunes: "White Christmas," "Canadian Capers," "Rudolph the Red-Nosed Raindeer." Outside, it was ninety degrees in the shade.

A few men my age were in the Dutchman's party. They had the look of guys that take cruises. Naturally the ones with their wives or girl-friends were no good to me. If I bagged one of those guys and took his visitor's pass, there was sure to be an awful squawk. Cruise ship wives may be out for a little cock, just like on the *Love Boat,* but they keep an eye on hubby all the time.

In spite of my tourist clothes and slightly ghoulish surveillance, I still wasn't sure I wanted to go through with it. *Try* to go through with it. They were all right, I was all wrong, a guy hustling for money in a strange country. I'd do it if there was no other way. Just the same, it stuck in my craw, the thought of leaving some poor guy stranded. Of course, he wouldn't be hurting for money. I'd leave him plenty, five thousand, maybe half of what I had. Ten thousand, to get out of these islands, was cheap.

A tall guy about forty came in and sat down at the Dutchman's table and got iced coffee. He had a bony, deeply tanned face and might be called handsome. Some of the ladies seemed to think so, because he got nearly as much attention as the Dutchman, though they didn't seem to know him. He had on a lightweight tan suit, a light gray shirt and a black tie. I don't know what he was, maybe the local agent of the cruise ship line. He wasn't sweating when he came in; that could mean he'd been in the islands for a long time, or was used to a hot climate. The Dutchman introduced him to some of the ladies and he bowed a little Teutonically, if that's the right word for how a Dutchman bows. I was too far away to hear his voice, but I figured him for a Dutchman, not that he had blond hair or any of the usual signs. His hair was black, with a little gray in it, just like mine. Yeah, I thought, just like mine.

One of the ladies who'd been rooting in her bag gave a yelp, as if she'd lost something. The officer and the other guy looked at her. Then she came over to their table and started to explain what the matter was. The officer smiled and patted her on the wrist. Whatever it was, it was no problem. The other man smiled too, and took a bunch of tickets from his wallet, selected one, asked the lady for her name, printed it on the ticket and signed his name. A visitor's pass. The lady had lost hers and now she had a new one.

The guy with the visitors' passes finished his coffee, nodded to the ladies and went out. I threw dollars on the table and followed him. The jukebox was playing skating music from a Sonja Henie movie. At the next corner, the guy with the tickets was talking to a cop. The cop was grinning, so nothing heavy was going down. Just a longtime foreign resident chatting with a cop he knew. A window crammed with souvenirs of Davao got all my attention until the tall guy waved to the cop and moved on. He was in no hurry. A lot of people seemed to know him, and he chatted or waved, a popular Dutchman.

Halfway down Rizal Street, he turned into a quieter street, then made another turn that took him into a little square lined on four sides with office buildings, banks, airline and tourist offices. He went into NETHERLANDS CRUISES and

135

when I walked by, I saw him talking to a blond woman behind the counter. In the plate glass window there were pictures of white ships, places with palm trees and happy tourists. I stopped to look at an enlarged color photograph of St. Croix. An artificial palm tree inside the window provided some cover. The Dutchman was sitting at a desk with his jacket off. Two other desks were unoccupied.

The center of the square was a small park, with trees, benches, a fountain that sent up a haze of water. Rainbows shimmered in the water. Men and women, mostly older people, sat on the benches; little kids ran in and out of the fountain. A peaceful scene.

There was nothing I could do at the moment. Sticking up the guy at his desk would bring every cop in Davao down on me. Besides, I had no idea when the cruise ship was going to sail. Maybe that evening, maybe tomorrow. Then I thought, suppose I knock the guy out and take his wallet, make it look like everyday mugger stuff? All seaports have muggers, even in the cop-heavy Philippines. The cops would ask him what was in the wallet and he'd tell them money, cards, ID, tourist passes. The uniformed men would pass the case along to the detectives. That was routine. The detectives wouldn't just pat him on the head and tell him they'd be in touch if anything turned up. He was a foreign resident of some importance, and a citizen of a highly regarded country, so they wouldn't just file and forget. There would be a complete investigation. The Dutchman was popular.

It depended on who got the case, how smart

he was. Money was the usual motive in a mugging; the visitor's passes would come next. If a regular cop, not a secret policeman, handled the squeal, he might not make the connection between the missing wallet and this American, Rainey. I didn't know. I just didn't know how it would go.

From where I was there was a good view of NETHERLANDS TOURS. A line of shrubs bordered the park, so I wasn't just sitting there with my fly open. The blond woman left, checking the lock before she closed the door behind her. A hooker came by and bothered me, a Japanese-Filipino with an American accent. I told her no sale, then she asked me for a cigarette. I said I didn't smoke and she said she was trying to kick the habit herself. Was I sure I didn't want "to go on a party?" Some other time, I said. Her last effort to do some kind of business was an offer to pay me a thousand dollars if I'd marry her and take her to the States.

"I'm married, with four kids," I said.

"You would be," she said. "Why is it the good guys are always tied up?"

I took a walk around the park, inspected some statues of dead heroes, then walked by NETHERLANDS TOURS with my hat off. The Dutchman was still at his desk, turned to one side, talking on the telephone. On the window, the office hours were given as eight to five. It was long after five and I couldn't stay in the park much longer. Tourists don't sit in parks with the natives. It's all right for a weary tourist to rest his feet; longer than that, it begins to look suspicious.

But I took a chance and made another round

of the park. Some of the Filipinos looked at me. I think some of them pegged me for a queer or a child molester, all those little kids running around. The hooker was still cruising the park, and she waved to me from a drinking fountain. A few minutes later, I saw her talking on the phone in an outdoor booth. I was coming up the street when the Dutchman came out.

I followed him to the International Cocktail Lounge on President Marcos Street, a few blocks from the park. He was at the bar drinking San Miguel when I came in and sat at a table close to a bunch of Americans who were drinking "island" drinks with blossoms sticking out of them. It was early and the place wasn't too crowded. The Americans were arguing about Mae West's birthdate.

"I say she was at least a hundred when she died," one guy said, positive as only a drunk can be.

"Naw. Naw. Naw," another clown said. "You're wrong, there, Skip. I would say she couldn't of been a day over, let me think, a day over eighty-eight. True, there's some dispute about the exact date she was born, but I would go for the eight-eight, all right, say ninety, figure." The Dutchman was talking to the bartender at his end of the bar.

"Hey, buddy," one of the Americans said to me. "Pardon us, we don't want to bother you, but maybe you can settle a little argument we've been having, okay?"

"Sure," I said. "What's the argument about?"

"Mae West," he said solemnly. "How old do you think she was when she passed away? Take your time now."

I pretended to think. The Dutchman was on his second beer. "Gee, I can't be sure," I said. "At the time I think I read the paper she was ninety-two. But please don't take my word for it."

This didn't satisfy everybody at the next table, but soon they forget about Mae West's age and began to do a recap of her movies. Film critics. Cinema scholars.

"Hey, why don't you pull up a chair?" one of them said. "I hate to see a guy drinking by himself."

I sat in. There were five of them, all from the Boston area. Skipper. Arnie. Johnny. Morris. Oscar. I was Alex Beaudry from Baton Rouge. The Dutchman was reading a newspaper the bartender had given him.

"You may not agree with me," Arnie said, "But I think *My Little Chickadee* was the funniest movie Mae West ever made." Arnie had thick glasses, a big nose, a flowered shirt. He was middle-aged but his gray hair, carefully cut, came down over his ears. "Mae West and W. C. Fields, what a combination! Remember the scene where W. C. Fields is in bed with the goat and he thinks it's Mae West because the lights are out and he starts getting horny and when the goat starts bleating W. C. Fields says something like, 'I love your little love cries, my sweet'? You remember that scene, Skipper?"

Skipper moved the blossoms to one side and took a swig of his "island" drink. "Yeah, I remember," he said, "only I missed the movie when it first came out. That was 1940, I think. What was I then? Fifteen, yeah. I caught it on TV a few years back and I thought it was pretty

139

funny."

"What do you mean, *pretty* funny," Arnie said. "It was hilarious!"

Skipper made a face. "They probably edited the shit out of it for TV."

Oscar was drunker than the others and hadn't been saying much. Now he said, "You guys don't know what you're talking about. The one with Mae West and Cary Grant in it was ten times funnier. The one where Mae West runs this big Bowery saloon, the Gay Nineties, and Cary Grant has this mission right down the street. Lloyd Nolan was the chief of police. Noah Beery, that's Wallace Beery's brother, plays some kind of Tammany Hall politician. Gilbert Roland was a gigolo. Yeah."

Skipper winked at the others. "Hey Oscar, how old are you, anyway? That movie was made in 1933, that's fifty years ago. You must've been at least twelve or thirteen to get into the movie. So what are you now? Sixty-two? Sixty-three?"

Everybody laughed, including Oscar. "Fuck you, Skipper, I'm the same age as you are, thirty-nine."

"We're all thirty-nine," the one named Morris said.

"I saw that movie at a revival house in Cambridge," Oscar said. "The Brattle, near Harvard Square, you know it?"

The Dutchman was still reading the paper. I wondered if he intended to sit and drink beer all evening. There was nothing I could do about it, if he did. Come to think of it, a guy with a skinful of beer might be a lot easier to handle.

The bar was starting to fill up. "Of course, we

know the Brattle," the one called Johnny said, a little peeved at Oscar's suggestion that he might not know it. "That's the dump where they keep showing *Casablanca* all the time. One time they showed it for a straight month. The potheads from Harvard can't get enough of it. They know every fucking line in the movie. They talk along with the dialogue, sing along when that colored guy plays the piano."

Oscar sucked in his drink, owl-eyed and happy. "Play it again, Sam," he said. "That was no colored guy, that was Hoagy Carmichael."

Skipper bristled. "Like hell it was. It was a colored guy and his name was Dooley Wilson. Am I right, Alex?"

I was Alex. "You're right," I said. "Hoagy Carmichael played a piano player in some other Bogart movie."

"I was in the Brattle once and I didn't like it," Johnny said. "It stank of pot and disinfectant. You couldn't hear the movie for all the shit that was going on. Those kids there are a bunch of yo-yo's."

Oscar signaled to the Filipino waiter. "The same again, *paisan*," he said. "Alex here, I don't know what he's having. A beer? Okay, a beer and the same again for the rest of us."

Skipper stared at Johnny. "Why're you always dumping on kids, huh? I have four kids and two of them're a bit wild, so what? They'll straighten out. So what were you when you were a kid? You think you were a fucking plaster saint or something? Maybe you don't remember the time we went joyriding in that guy's car and wrapped it around a lamp pole. We'd of been in the shit if Arnie's father wasn't

141

a rabbi and talked to the owner and the cops. Your old man came through for us, Arnie, God rest his soul."

"Nobody's dumping on *all* kids," Johnny protested. "Did you hear me saying your kids aren't okay? I'm talking about these wiseass Harvard fuckers. Some of them aren't even kids. I'm talking about these professional students, some of them bald even, they're that fucking *old.* It's guys like that break my balls. How do they live? Off the taxpayer, that's how. Grants. Welfare. Public assistance."

"Some of them have rich parents," Arnie said.

"That's just as bad," Johnny said. Johnny looked Italian, stocky, talky, tough. A guy who had worked his way up to a string of pizza parlors, a busy undertaker's business, a round-the-clock used car lot? Now in middle age, they all had money, and I wondered where their wives were.

"You have any kids, Alex?" Skipper wanted to know.

"I'm not married," I told him.

Skipper winked. "You don't have to be married to have kids. You know, you're the smartest guy at this table. Why do I make that statement? Because you never got married, that's why. You never put your head in a noose like the rest of us. Man, what I wouldn't give to be not married!"

"Get a divorce." That was Oscar's contribution. "A divorce is no big thing these days."

Skipper shook his head, regretting what might have been. "How can I get a divorce when the business is in my fucking wife's name? That's what happens to you when you screw around with the IRS. But if I *could* get a divorce, Jesus Christ, I wouldn't know what to do with myself. I'd be like a cat in a dairy, a wolf in with a bunch of lambs. I'd probably screw myself to death in six months. But what a way to go, right? I'd get myself a nice apartment right in Boston—fuck the suburbs—and fix it up just right. I wouldn't keep a stick of furniture from the house in Waltham, and I wouldn't give it to Morgan Memorial or Goodwill, because that fucking furniture has a jinx on it. A curse!"

I don't know what they put in those island drinks; it must have been pretty good. Skipper was in good voice and he wanted to be heard. The others were enjoying it, and only Arnie, the serious guy in the group, tried to make him see the good side of married life.

"Look Skip," he said. "I know you and Marie don't get along, but you have your kids. How can you say nothing good came out of your marriage? How can you say it?"

"I like the kids, I *love* the kids," Skipper said. "Marie I hate. Hate. *Hate.* Hate with all my heart and soul. If I thought I'd get away with it, I'd hire a hit man. Five thousand. Ten thousand. What's the difference, if it guarantees peace of mind? I can't sleep nights. My stomach is going back on me. Where is it written that a guy has to suffer in Purgatory while he's still on earth? Answer me that, Arnie? Arnie, the deep thinker."

"Tell us about your apartment." Morris said.

Skipper looked at him, puzzled. "What apartment?"

"The one you're going to get in downtown

Boston."

"Fat chance I'll ever get to do it. Hey, maybe Marie the ball-buster will drop dead of a heart attack, get run over by a truck. You remember the time the plate glass window kept falling out of that new insurance building they were building? People got hurt, I think at least one killed. Why couldn't it have been Marie?"

The Dutchman left his half-finished beer and went to a booth in back to make a phone call. It was a short call, less than three minutes. On the way out, he stopped at the bar to drink the rest of his beer.

"Hey Alex, what's your hurry?" Skipper called after me.

NINE

I followed the Dutchman to a new apartment building on Quezon Avenue, a stark white high-rise with expensive cars parked out front. Most of them were Japanese and German; a DeLorean, shiny new, was being towed away by a garage truck. The Dutchman went in and waited for one of the elevators. I waited too. The Dutchman glanced at me the way you might glance at any stranger. A fat Filipino in an ice cream suit joined us, fanning his heated face with his panama hat.

We got on and the Dutchman pressed the button for 17. "What floors, gentlemen?" he said.

I said, "Seventeen;" the Filipino wanted ten.

After the Filipino got off, the Dutchman smiled and said, "There's no need for the gun, Mr. Rainey. I want to talk to you, you want to talk to me. So there's no need for the gun. I have a gun too, but it's still in its holster."

"Okay," I said.

We got off and I followed him into a big

breezy apartment in which everything seemed to be white. Sliding glass doors that led to a balcony were open; white fiberglass curtains blew in the breeze; up so high, street traffic was a murmur.

The Dutchman took off his jacket, exposing a soft leather shoulder holster without a chest strap. "It's a Walther PPK," he said. "What are you carrying?"

"Regulation Colt forty-five," I said. "You want to see it?"

"I'll take your word for it. Sit down. Do you want a drink? I have everything. I'm going to have a beer. You'll have a beer? Good."

He'd been onto me all the time. Whatever he was, he was no travel agent. What was he, then?

There was no bar in the living room, and I thought that showed class He got beer and glasses from the kitchen, then set everything down on a glass-topped table between two white crushed-leather couches. The glasses were tall, thin and frosted; he poured beer for me.

"I'm security for Netherlands Tours," he said. "In Davao, that is. I spotted you in that silly ice cream parlor. You didn't look as if you belonged, but that was just a passing thought. Then you followed me. I saw you when I was chatting with that policeman and you were so engrossed with that shop window. Too engrossed. You may be a bang-up mercenary, but you're not cut out for undercover work. Too tall, for one thing."

I drank some beer. "All right, you spotted me.

How do you know who I am?"

"The secret police told me." He took a long drink of beer and smacked his lips. A beer lover. "They told me to keep a lookout for an American, James Rainey, who might try to sneak onto my cruise ship. A matter of national security, they said. Top secret. Burn before reading, and so on. Secret policemen are so secretive. My instructions were to check all my tourists, to make certain you didn't knock some fellow on the head and take his visitor's pass. That was why you followed those idiotic tourists, wasn't it?"

"I was thinking about it," I said, still not getting it. If he planned to turn me over to the secret police, then why the beer and the chat?

"You changed your mind when you saw me making out a new pass for that woman. Aha, you thought, here's a fellow with a whole pocketfull of passes. I'll steal his wallet and he and the police will think I did it just for the money. Not a bad plan at that, but what about the diary? On the ship, you'd be discovered sooner or later. Stowaways usually are. When they found you, they'd find the diary. Or hadn't you thought that far ahead?"

"I might have thrown the diary overboard, I might have given it to the captain. If the secret police didn't tell you much, how do you know about the diary? How do you know I'm a mercenary?"

"Because I checked with Dutch Intelligence," the Dutchman said. "My name is Martin Van Dalen, by the way. Oh yes, Dutch Intelligence still maintains a presence in this part of the world. Holland is a small country, true, but even a small country likes to think it's important."

"Then you're not just a security man for a cruise ship company?"

"Yes, indeed I am. It's a fine job and I wouldn't think of changing. But I do pass along useful information to our intelligence service. Professional courtesy. I don't even take money for it. Not worth the niggardly amounts they pay. I called Manila and they called Interpol. You have a dossier, Mr. Rainey. Nothing really criminal in it, but Interpol does keep an eye on you. My friends in Intelligence called me back and said the Manila underworld was buzzing with rumors about you and a diary kept by the late General Clifford Sanders. A secret diary dealing with some conspiracy to betray the Philippines just before the war. My friends were a bit vague about it, perhaps intentionally, and I'm not even sure they believe in the diary's existence."

"What else did they say?"

"I'm coming to that, the most interesting part. Several Americans new to the islands have been asking questions about you. Thugs with plenty of money and willing to pay for information. That was about a week ago. They could be anywhere by now. Perhaps you know who they are?"

"Maybe," I said.

"There's no need to be so reticent," Van Dalen said. "I'm going to help you and you're going to pay me well."

"Am I?"

"Of course you are. You're in a tight spot and

you need me to get you out of it. The secret police are after you, so are these American thugs." He paused, leaning forward with the air of a man about to spring a surprise. "You have no way of knowing that Mrs. Sanders was murdered shortly after you left Manila."

"I know about it," I said.

That raised his eyebrows. "Indeed? Well, we won't go into that at the moment. The secret police may have murdered the old lady, but I'm inclined to think the Americans did it. Mrs. Sanders was tortured before she was killed, but I don't think it was the work of the secret police, because they prefer to conduct their investigations"—Van Dalen smiled—"in the cellars underneath police headquarters. So I cast my vote for the Americans. Do you agree or disagree?"

"I don't disagree," I said.

"Do you have any reason to think the diary isn't authentic?"

I shook my head.

"Neither do the police or the Americans. That means it's worth a great deal of money. How much I can't even guess at."

"And you want part of it?"

"Oh, no. I'm tempted, of course, but the answer to that is no."

"I don't believe you."

"Why not? If I wanted the diary, would we be here talking?" He pointed to the airline bag; it was on couch beside me. "It's in that silly bag, but I don't want it. Good God, no! You may be killed at any moment because of it. Do you think I want to put myself in the same position? Thanks but no thanks."

149

I didn't know what to make of this guy. "Then what the hell *do* you want?"

"The money Mrs. Sanders paid you. Your Interpol file says you never work except for big money. The rumor is that you got a hundred thousand dollars for bringing that American journalist out of Afghanistan."

"Mrs. Sanders didn't pay me anything like that."

"But it must have been a considerable amount." Van Dalen looked hopeful.

"I got paid enough," I said. "Come on, what are you really up to? We both have guns, but I think I can shoot you before you can shoot me."

Van Dalen stood up, but all he did was go to the kitchen for more beer. "You have to get guns out of your head," he said, coming back.

"I don't figure you," I said. "You look like a crook, you talk like a crook, so what goes on?"

Van Dalen filled my glass with beer. "A crook, but a small crook," he said. "I was a big-time crook when I was a detective inspector in Amsterdam. Not any more. I was reckless then. Blame it on youth—not that I was so very young when they caught me. I was attached to the waterfront section. That's where the real money is, in Amsterdam. Dope from the Far East: heroin, hash, hash oil, opium for the older generation of dopers. Holland has been associated with the Far East for so long. Next to Marseilles, Amsterdam is the biggest drug port in Europe. Working with friends in Customs, I got rich. Very rich. I was just a policemen, yet I was able to go to Cannes and sleep with movie starlets."

"But you got caught."

"By the sheerest chance. An act of God. I don't see how you can call it anything else. We had it so well organized, there seemed no way of finding us out. How was I to know my closest associate would be diagnosed as having inoperable cancer? Anyway, the wretched bastard went back to the church determined to cleanse his soul before he died. Part of his repentance included going to the police commissioner and telling all."

"How come you're here and not in jail? Or did you do time and get out?"

The memory of his ordeal made Van Dalen sweat a little. He picked up the cold beer bottle and rolled it across his forehead. Then he set it down and loosened his tie. His nervousness seemed real enough.

"Luckily for me, the cancerous bastard died while the commissioner was still digging in the dirt. He was the only witness. Without his evidence, they could hardly put me on trial. I think the commissioner was as glad to see him go as the rest of us. Big names were involved—shipping executives, ships' officers, a politician or two. But I had to resign, just the same."

It might all be a pack of lies. "How'd you got this job with a background like that?"

"My friends in the shipping business. They wanted to take care of me because they knew I wouldn't talk even if I got sent to prison. Then, too, they wanted me as far from Holland as I could get. My first choice was Hong Kong, but the British wouldn't have me, after they checked my record. The Philippine authorities weren't so fussy, so here I am. I have a good job, I still do a little business on the side, but I'm older and wiser now and very discreet in my choice of associates."

"Like the secret police?"

"Everyone in security has to get along with the police. Certainly I give them information from time to time. Why not?"

"You say you don't want trouble. I could be a lot worse trouble than protecting dope smugglers."

"I don't see why you have to be. I won't tell and you won't tell. I don't know what's in the diary and I don't want to know. Too rich for my blood. But I do need money—you see this apartment. My mistress likes nice things—I'm sure we can do business. I'm not a bigtime crook any longer, Mr. Rainey. I just want to get along and not make waves. In a few years I'd like to retire, go to Baguio—that's a lovely mountain resort in Luzon—and join the foreign colony there. I have British friends there. People sometimes take me for British. I spent two years in Britain as part of a police exchange program . . ."

"You haven't said what you're going to do for me," I interrupted.

"Oh!" Van Dalen looked surprised. "Why, get you on my cruise ship, of course. I thought that was understood. You can't use your own passport, naturally, so you'll have to have another. No problem there. In my work, I come into possession of many passports. People lose them, and so on."

"You're in the phony documents business?"

"I dabble," Van Dalen said, no longer nervous. "Anyway, just so it looks right, tomorrow morning, early, you will come to Netherlands

Tours and ask if there's any possibility of joining the *Wilhelmina* for the rest of the cruise. She will refer you to me and I will say, why yes, there is a vacant cabin formerly occupied by Mr. and Mrs. Peters of New York. That will be the truth: Mr. Peters came down with a strangulated hernia and had to be hospitalized in Cape Town."

"Sounds good," I said.

"Yes, it does, but we haven't settled the money part of it. How much did Mrs. Sanders pay you?"

"Ten thousand as a down payment, fifteen thousand when I delivered the diary."

Van Dalen frowned. "That seems awfully small for a man like you. Ten thousand! I think it must have been more like twenty-five, the down payment. Interpol says . . ."

"Never mind what Interpol says. General Sanders was just an army officer. All right, he left his widow comfortably off, not rolling in money. She told me all she could afford was twenty-five thousand, ten to be paid up front. That's the truth."

"I'll be taking an awful chance for only ten thousand," Van Dalen said.

"You mean you want all of it?"

"All of it, and it isn't enough."

"I'll give you seventy-five hundred. I'm going to need money to get home."

"You don't need that much to get home. You don't need any money at all. Mr. and Mrs. Peters' fare was paid in advance. No refunds just because a passenger has to leave the ship. You can stay aboard and get back to New York for nothing."

I didn't want to push him too hard on the money. "Okay, you get nine thousand and I keep a thousand for spending money."

"Five hundred, take it or leave it," Van Dalen said.

"Okay," I said. "You'll get the money as soon as I get the passport and the ticket. How do I get to travel for nothing, by the way?"

"Arrangements will be made with the purser. Don't concern yourself with that. Money talks. Now I'm going to take your picture. The wall behind you will do nicely."

Van Dalen got a camera and took my picture, using the blank white wall as background.

"What time should I come to the office?" I asked, picking up the airline bag.

Van Dalen looked at the bag and his face got a little greedy. I hoped greed wouldn't win out over caution. I believed him when he said he wanted to stay with the smalltime rackets. Even so, the diary was worth an awful lot of money and he might get to dreaming of one last big score.

"Be there at eight-thirty," he said. "Just in case the girl is a few minutes later. I want her as a witness, not that there should be the slightest bit of bother. Now, if you don't mind, I have to change. An important dinner date, you know."

I hoped Van Dalen's finagling wasn't going to be the death of him. He was a man who couldn't make up his mind what he wanted to be. The threat of a long jail term had scared the shit out of him, but not enough to make him go straight. There are people like that, and for all his caution, I felt pretty sure that Van Dalen wasn't going to make it as far as the country club set in Baguio.

I went back to my waterfront hotel room after stopping to eat in a Chinese restaurant. My tourist disguise must have been pretty good; no one even looked at me. I brought beer up to the room, sat under the sun umbrella on the balcony, and checked to see what was happening down at the MacGregor Company boats. The *MacGregory 5,* nearly loaded by now, was still there, and so were the uniformed police.

I was on my second bottle of beer, when the crew of the cargo ship began to straggle back from the town. Most of them had a load on, but they walked straight enough. Australians can drink. The first mate was down on deck; the captain kept an eye on things from the bridge. After a while, the captain called down to the mate. The mate shook his head and kept looking at the hilly street that came down to the docks. He yelled up to the captain when he saw the black Mercedes.

Thirty minutes later, after another search of the ship, the *MacGregor 5* was allowed to sail. A police patrol boat followed it out into the harbor, then turned back. The three timber boats started their engines and headed back upriver. I drank the rest of the beer.

Launches came and went from the cruise ship, the *Wilhelmina.* Some of the tourists going out had armloads of souvenirs. The officers in charge of the tourists were as blond and handsome as the first guy I'd seen. Tomorrow, if all went well, I'd be part of the gang.

I went over my deal with Van Dalen and couldn't find any holes in it. After the Dutchman was paid off, I'd still have ten thousand, not much money for what I'd been through, but better than nothing. The money didn't matter a damn; I just wanted to get home. Far from being a straight assignment, this one had been a fuck-up from the word go. First, Mrs. Sanders had lied to me about the diary. Then, to really screw things up, she had been tortured and murdered, and I couldn't have been in Mindanao more than a day when the people who killed her knew all about me. No more working for lying old ladies, I decided.

Cruise ships must be the biggest bore imaginable, and yet I was looking forward to quiet days at sea, with plenty of warm sun and cold beer. At night, I'd probably read a book in one of the bars until it was time to go to bed. There would be plenty of available broads on board, but I was going to give them a miss. I like my broads to be in places I can walk out if they start coming on too heavy, start asking too many questions.

In the morning, I'd get a schedule of ports of call from Van Dalen, then decide where I was going to get off. The thought of going the whole cruise made me cringe. I wondered if the *Wilhelmina* put in at any of the Australian ports. If I got off in, say, Sydney, I could fly out the same day. New Zealand was just as good as Australia; in all the other Asian countries there could be problems.

It got dark and there were lights down in the harbor. A hooter sounded as a freighter put out to sea. I wondered if the secret police were still torturing the Cuban. Maybe one bunch of torturers went home and another took over. The

Cuban would never get out of there alive, and even if he survived the beating and the burning, the electrodes attached to his balls, there would be no jail time for him, just a bullet in the head. That could be me down there in the cells under police headquarters, I thought. And I still could end up there if I didn't watch myself every minute.

The hotel was dirty and rundown and had no air conditioning; I'd taken a room there only because I could watch the harbor from the balcony in back of it. It was too hot and too early to sleep; eight-thirty was a long time to wait.

A bunch of sailors and whores came up from the lobby and went into the next room. The sailors were French and one of them was singing "Goin' to Jackson," the Johnny Cash song, in French. One of the whores or sailors carried a radio with a big sound; it got bigger as soon as they got into the room and turned it up. The walls were thin and the rattle of bottles and glasses being set down came through. Everything the Frenchmen said was funny to the whores; they laughed all the time. The party got louder as the liquor went down. I went out.

Rizal Street, the main drag, was going good when I got up to it. Tourists were everywhere, mostly men at that time of night, and on many of their faces was the grim look you see in men determined to have a good time no matter how hard they have to work at it. I came to GI Joe's and went in to get a drink.

GI Joe was still there kidding the customers and watching the bartenders. "Then there was the Frenchman who got his first look at his new mistress, a really buxom broad. 'Mon Dieu,' said the Frenchman. 'Is that all for me?' " GI Joe waited for the laughter to subside before he started on another joke. His jokes were old, but he kept them short, and the customers seemed to like that as much as the jokes themselves. GI Joe charged plenty for his drinks; maybe he thought of himself as a floor show.

But it was just a bar and I didn't mind it. There were more Americans than Filipinos. A very young hooker came in and GI Joe chased her out, saying, "Every American is entitled to life, liberty and the pursuit of young girls, but I'd rather they did it in the privacy of their bedroom and not in my bar." GI put on a bad Southern accent. "Ah runs a respeckabul place heah and don' want nobody a-messin' it up."

"Have a heart, Joe," an elderly American with a baseball cap said. "Let the poor kid come in and I'll buy her a cherry Coke."

That was the signal for a joke about girls losing their cherries. The old fellow in the baseball cap must have heard it many times before, but he laughed as hard as the first time. "You slay me, Joe," he said, wheezing with merriment.

"You think I'm hep?" GI Joe had to know.

"Right arm," the old fellow said.

I had two more drinks, standing at the bar because all the tables were occupied, and when more people came in and it got too crowded, I took a walk down Rizal Street. Down the street, two uniformed cops were putting handcuffs on a drunk who had broken a liquor store window with an empty wine bottle. One of the runty cops, a very dark Filipino, got mad and whacked the bum across the kidneys with his stick. The bum fell down and began to scream; to shut him up, the two cops kicked him in the head.

I bought sandwiches, beer and newspapers in a grocery store on a side street, then started back toward the hotel. The party next door had to end some time. If it didn't, I would just have to put up with it. It didn't much matter if I couldn't sleep. Plenty of time to sleep on the ship, I thought.

To get back to the hotel I had to stay on the street that led to the docks. There were lights, but it seemed dark after the glare of Rizal Street. Down the hill, two of the streetlights had burned out or been knocked out. Just to be safe, I got off the sidewalk and walked in the middle of the narrow street. A car came up the hill and turned the corner. No car traffic after that, and no people. I kept on going, holding the bag of groceries in the crook of my left arm. My right hand stayed close to the .45 stuck inside my belt. The street didn't seem any more dangerous than a thousand other streets in the Philippines. I'd know in a minute.

I dropped the groceries and yanked out the .45 when I heard them coming up behind.

TEN

Two young Chinese sprang forward swinging leather covered saps, but they weren't trying to kill me. Not yet anyway. They wanted to make sure I had the diary or could tell them where it was. The .45 was on safety and ready to fire as soon as I snapped it off. Working the slide can take time, and I didn't have time. I shot the first one in the chest and he died on his feet. His companion brought his sap down on my gun arm and I felt it go dead. The .45 clattered into half-darkness as the sap whistled straight at my head. I dodged the swing and brought him down with a flying tackle, but not doing so good because of my arm. He snarled and tried to bite at my face. I smashed him in the face with my forehead and blood spattered from his broken nose. For a moment I thought he'd hit me with the sap, but it was just the shock of my own blow. We rolled all over the street, covered with blood and panting like brutes. My head was clearing and when we rolled again I felt the .45 under me. I tried to grab it and he used that to break my hold and get on top of me, still gripping the sap and trying to get in a swing that would knock me out. The sap came down and I took the blow in the palm of my hand. Then my hand closed on the sap before he could jerk it away. Our faces were close together and I could smell the grease in his hair, the sweat of his unwashed body. We fought silently, fiercely, knowing one of us had to die. Then we rolled back over the .45 and this time I got it. His hand closed on my wrist, but I was stronger than he was; inch by inch, the gun came up close to his heart. There was pain as his long fingernails dug into my wrist. I squeezed the trigger. A .45 is a big round to take anywhere in the body, but this murderous son of a bitch was still kicking when I moved the .45 and fired again. The second bullet, fired straight into his heart, killed him instantly.

I went down the hill at a staggering run, holding the airline bag by the strap. Up above a siren wailed, but the police car hadn't turned the corner yet. It was too far to the hotel to make it without being seen. An old car with two flat tires was the only cover I saw and I was still trying to crawl under it when the headlights of the cop car lit up the street and the siren wound down to silence. Doors slammed; I heard the crackle of the police radio. From under the car I could see them looking at the bodies. Two Filipino cops, the driver and his partner. One got back in the car to talk on the radio, the other went through the pockets of the dead men, probably looking for money. Cops are cops: if the cops don't get a dead man's money, the ambulance boys will. A fact of life in any city.

Another police car arrived; this one had plain-clothes men in it. Next came the ambulance. It took the bodies away while the cops stayed there talking. Then they came down the hill, stopping short of where I was. There are badass Chinese gangs in the Philippines, just like New York, and maybe these cops weren't ready to die because of two dead Chinks in a dark back street. I stayed where I was, holding the .45, ready to open fire if they changed their minds and started to poke around the car. At least I'd die fast. Anything was better than being turned over to the secret police. Finally they got back in their cars and went away.

I gave it another thirty minutes before I crawled out and went down the hill to look at myself under a street light. My shirt was ruined, but I had a clean one in the bag, and I put it on. I wiped my face and hands with the dirty shirt and after that I didn't look too bad. What I hoped I looked like was a tourist who'd gotten drunk and taken a few falls. This was the dock area, after all, and some of the guys I'd seen at the hotel didn't look any better than I did.

The desk clerk was reading a magazine when I came in. One bored look was all I got. I wondered if the men I'd killed had any connection with the Chinese guerrilla with the limp. My arm was still hurt from the blow from the sap, but it wasn't broken. I showered under rusty-looking water, then washed out the pants and hung them by the window to dry. The party in the next room was down to a few grunts and giggles. I was too tired to care. If the cops came to search the hotel, then so be it.

It stayed quiet for the rest of the night. Going

out, the French sailors woke me up. By then it was about six and I'd slept enough. My arm hurt like a bastard. It was badly discolored just above the elbow, but it worked all right. The pants were dry and I dressed after I shaved and showered. In another hour I'd shove off to keep my appointment with the Dutchman.

On the way, I ate breakfast in a small restaurant with a uniformed cop sitting on a counter stool. He was more interested in his sausages and eggs than he was in me. A police car passed and the cop at the counter looked at it in the mirror and made some joke to the waitress. I didn't know what he said to her.

I sat at a table by the window and ordered a ham steak and eggs. The place was Filipino, but the influences were all American right down to the "funny" signs taped to the wall behind the counter. A wall clock said seven-thirty and I knew that was right because I'd seen another clock on my way up from the hotel. I needed to buy a wristwatch, but that could wait for the ship.

The ship? Maybe the ship was going to be all right. It depended on how reliable Van Dalen was. But once I was aboard and the ship had sailed, there wasn't much he could do. He couldn't confess his sins to the secret police or even try to sell them a story of how he'd been stuck up and forced to help me escape. No, if he didn't betray me today, it would be too late tomorrow.

Getting the diary on board wouldn't be a problem. Tourists in the Philippines don't have to file a customs declaration and are usually exempt from customs examinations. They may check you coming in, but they hardly ever do it going out. That keeps the tourists happy; it's good public relations.

The diary, in the bag, lay on the seat beside me. Van Dalen was convinced that I was going to sell it. Any crook would laugh if I told him otherwise. I could probably sell it to one of the New York or London tabloids. How much? Five hundred thousand? Was that too much or too little? I was no expert in the sale of hot diaries. MacArthur got a lot of space in the diary, right up to the time Truman fired him for talking back about crossing the Yalu River. Why hadn't MacArthur done anything about the conspiracy? According to Sanders, the men named in the diary continued to hold high office or high rank throughout the war and long afterward. There was no doubt in my mind that there had been a conspiracy. Military intelligence could have unraveled it if MacArthur had given the order. Sanders said he just wasn't interested. Why not?

MacArthur had been a towering figure in the Philippines before the war; when he retired from the U.S. Army in the mid-1930's, President Quezon created a new rank for him as commander in chief of the Philippine armed forces: field marshal. This announcement was greeted with cynical laughter back in the States, but MacArthur wore his field marshal's gold sunburst without a trace of embarrassment. There was a little dictator in old Mac and the Philippines suited him well. He was taller than most Filipinos and they looked up to him in more ways than one. He failed to stop the Jap invasion, but when he vowed to return, he did.

Admiral Leahy tried to persuade FDR to bypass the Philippines, which most military experts agree would have been the smartest thing to do, but MacArthur had to have his "return," and he did. But why hadn't he even checked out General Sanders' findings? He had the apparatus to do it . . . What the hell! That was more than forty years ago and I had an appointment in thirty minutes.

I got to NETHERLANDS TOURS at eight-twenty. The blond girl was behind the counter, Van Dalen at his desk. I went in, asked about getting a place on the cruise ship, and was sent over to talk to Van Dalen, who shook hands and looked businesslike. There was no one else in the office.

Van Dalen overplayed it a bit, but then his normal manner, if you could call it that, was slightly stagy. "Why yes, it just so happens that we have a vacancy," he said in his Dutch-British accent. "An American couple had to leave the ship at Cape Town. Husband became ill, poor chap, and had to be hospitalized. We have a highly qualified doctor aboard ship, but, of course, there are limits to what can be done at sea."

I sat there listening to all this. "How soon can I go aboard?"

"As soon as your ticket is ready and I've checked your passport. Your passport is in order, Mr. De Pauw? Yes, I'm sure it is. Miss Stryjom, will you be so good as to get us some coffee? This is going to take a few minutes."

The blond girl went out and Van Dalen took a U.S. passport from his inside pocket and handed it to me. In it, my name was given as

Willem Erik De Pauw; I had been born in Ana-heim, California, in 1945. Everything, description and photograph, matched up fine. I couldn't find any fault with the Passport Office seal. The passport had a slightly worn look, as if it had been to a lot of places, and I could see why when I flipped through it and studied the visas and immigration stamps.

"What am I?" I asked.

"You're a retired U.S. Army officer . . . no, make that an army officer who's come into money . . . a dead uncle . . . and you've been traveling and enjoying life ever since. You look like an ex-soldier and it's best to stick to what you know. That way you won't find yourself talking to some salesman about things you know nothing about. Not that it matters much. The passport and visas will pass all but the closest inspection. It's to my interest that you not be caught."

"My interest too."

"The money?"

I handed him the ninety-five hundred and he counted it quickly, then put it in his pocket. Then the girl was coming in with two containers of coffee and Van Dalen was saying, his voice theatrical again, "I'm sure you'll have a marvelous time, Mr. De Pauw. Have you sailed with us before? Ah, here's Miss Stryjom now. We'll enjoy our coffee while she makes out your ticket."

I drank my coffee while he went to the counter and gave Miss Stryjom instructions. She might have been in on it, for all I knew. It was hard to see how he could work it if she wasn't in on it. Maybe she was doing it for love.

I thought I detected little hints of intimacy behind their boss-employee manner. Van Dalen came back to his desk.

"You'll find one of the ship's launches at Pier Twelve," he told me. "There won't be the slightest problem getting on board. You will have a cabin to yourself, so you won't have to share it or answer stupid questions. My advice is to remain on the ship for the rest of the voyage. That's not so unusual and the officers will think nothing of it. Cruise ships' officers have seen everything there is to see. Nothing surprises them." Van Dalen lowered his voice even more. "What have you been doing with your clothes? Sleeping in the streets? Oh well, there's a fine men's shop on board."

"I'd like to know where we put in after Davao," I said.

"A list will be attached to your ticket," Van Dalen said. "It will be ready in a moment."

The blond girl brought the ticket over, then went back to the counter. Van Dalen saw me looking at the list of ports of call and said quickly, "I'll walk out with you, Mr. De Pauw. I must make a call at the bank."

We walked away from the glass front of NETHERLANDS TOURS. Across the street, the park was bright green in the sun. Little kids ran in and out of the whirling fountain.

"Why didn't you tell me the next two ports of call are Zamboanga and Manila?" I said. "You knew that long before last night and you didn't tell me."

"What difference does it make? You won't be going ashore." Van Dalen was nervous, but doing his best to appear calm. "The call at

168

Zamboanga will be twelve hours; at Manila, twenty-four. Stay in your cabin, read, drink, watch cable films, screw a beautiful rich widow. Just don't go ashore. Come to think of it, you probably could go ashore and get away with it."

"I don't want to go ashore."

"Then don't."

"What if the police come on board?"

"For what reason? It's not as if the *Wilhelmina* were some grubby freighter with a cargo of hashish hidden in the hold. We've never had any trouble with the Philippine police. No reason why they should bother us now."

"They could decide to search all ships coming north from Davao."

"I'm telling you they won't search my ship. The *Wilhelmina* isn't our only ship: there are three others and they all call at Philippine ports. We bring in millions and the Marcos government needs the goodwill. They won't search the ship."

We were close to the corner. "I'm glad you're so certain," I said.

He shrugged. "I'm as certain as I can be. Rainey, if you don't want to go, give me back the passport and ticket, I'll charge you for expenses, and that's the end of it. But I can tell you this. You won't find a better way out."

He had me and he knew it. There was no better way to escape from the islands. Zamboanga and Manila were dangerous points; all I could do was take a chance and see what happened. Van Dalen waited for my answer, confident that I wasn't going to change the deal.

"Okay," I said. "We'll let it stand as it is. How

do I get to Pier Twelve from here?"

"Here's a taxi now," Van Dalen said, raising his hand. The taxi stopped and Van Dalen turned and walked away. He went into a bank on the corner, to deposit the ninety-five hundred, I suppose.

"Pier Twelve," I told the driver, a skinny Filipino with a leather vest and leather cap. He didn't look like any kind of cop, but you never know. A few quick looks in the rearview mirror didn't have to mean anything. Most taxi drivers do that. He didn't talk, for which I was thankful. He crossed Rizal Street, made a right, then a left, and Pier Twelve was at the end of the hill. A launch from the ship was letting off passengers; the cruise ship, tall and white, looked a lot closer.

I walked along with tourists going out to the ship on the empty launch. Two Filipino customs officers sitting in a wooden hut took no notice as we passed. A Dutch ship's officer and a civilian were talking in front of another hut.

"I was told to report here before going aboard," I said, holding up my passport.

The civilian, a white-skinned Eurasian, looked through the passport before he looked at me. Then he took the passport into the hut and stamped it. He had lost interest in me before he handed it back. The Dutchman asked me if I had my ticket, and I gave it to him.

"Welcome aboard, Mr. De Pauw," he said, giving me that friendly, not quite naval salute these guys use. "Please check in with the purser and he will attend to your needs."

The *Wilhelmina* was smaller than the *QE2,*

but not by much. We went out in the launch and it got bigger by the minute. It looked like a huge white hotel set down in deep blue water. No rustbucket this, its white paintwork glared in the morning sun. A freighter putting out to sea looked like a spavined nag beside the sleek Dutch thoroughbred. I'd been on lots of ships in my time, but never on a cruise ship. Some people made fun of cruise ships, but I didn't even grin at this one. It was my safe passage home—maybe. It was my ark in dark waters—maybe. From the start of this job, everything had been maybe.

I looked at the other passengers in the launch. Most of them were men that looked as if they'd spent the night in town, touring the whorehouses and bars, doing things they only read about in dirty books back home. There was that shamefaced look that is part hangover, part guilt. One naughty old boy took a surreptitious swig from a silver flask. Some of these guys were going to catch hell when they got back to the ship; I guess they figured it was worth it. The Dutchman in charge of the launch didn't have much to say, and maybe it was too early. As we rode out past the mouth of the harbor, the air was full of sea smells, salt and kelp and wet shells, and it was good to get away from the hot stink of the town. The launch climbed and dipped in the heavy swell; a thin cold spray was carried aft on the wind, and the old fellow who'd been nipping began to look green. He sat down on a wooden bench and mopped at his face with a small pack of Kleenex. In a few minutes, the launch cut its speed and the great white ship loomed over us.

"My wife is going to kill me," the old guy with the green face said to me. "Absolutely slaughter me, that's what she's going to do."

I shrugged and said nothing.

"Nobody has any sympathy these days," the old guy said. "It's a dog-eat-dog world out there."

There was a floating dock with a gangway going up to the ship; climbing aboard was a small adventure for the few ladies among us. One fortyish broad with copper streaks in her hair seemed to think I should help her. I didn't. Her man-eating smile, directed at me, was turned on the Dutch officer, who did his duty by the lady and the cruise ship company.

I went up and asked a steward where I could find the purser, and he said he'd show me the way. The purser was in his office drinking coffee and checking a list with a pencil. I gave him my passport and ticket, explaining that everything had been cleared with Van Dalen.

"Yes," he said. "He's been on the radio phone. You're in Cabin 54. Is that all the luggage you have?"

I hefted the airline bag. "I travel light. Mr. Van Dalen says there are shops on board."

"You can get anything you want on this ship, Mr. De Pauw. Here's a directory. You'll find a program of the ship's recreation facilities in your cabin. If there's anything special you want, just give me a ring."

I thought he gave me an odd look, but that could have been my imagination. After you've been hunted too long you begin to suspect everyone. It can run away with you if you don't put a curb on it.

I thanked him and went to my cabin. It was big and white and looked like a ship without having a lot of pipes sticking out of the walls. A small refrigerator was well stocked with Amstel beer, pickled onions, packaged cold cuts, orange juice, ice.

I opened a beer and lay down and drank from the bottle. The air-conditioning was up too high and I fixed that when I got up to get another beer. It was about ten; the ship was scheduled to sail at noon. Two more hours and I'm on my way, I thought. Zamboanga was the next port of call, and to get there we'd have to sail clear around the southern end of Mindanao. That was about five hundred miles, maybe more, and I hadn't asked the purser because the more questions you ask, the more people remember about you. I wanted to be Mr. Nobody on this trip, just a quiet American of Dutch descent taking a cruise for no particular reason.

When the passengers got through gawking at Zamboanga for twelve hours, we would sail north into the Sulu Sea, then past the island of Mindoro, arriving in Manila about a day later. My calculations were far from exact; it didn't matter; I was in for at least a thousand mile voyage.

The door was locked and I lay there until I heard the rattle of anchor chains. Then there was shouting and the ship's horn sounded, drowning out the goodbye music of the ship's band. Gentle vibrations shook the ship and it began to move. When I looked out the porthole, I saw Davao receding in the distance. Far behind it was the mountains rolling back as far as the eye could see. I couldn't see the big river

I had come down. Everything looked so peaceful, but out there a savage war was going on. My only thought was that I was glad to see the last of it.

I slept and when I woke up in the late afternoon, we were out of sight of land. Then I went to the men's shop and bought five hundred dollars' worth of good clothes—slacks, shirts, two cord jackets, socks and loafers. My aviator sunglasses were scratched from the fight with the Chinese killer, and I bought a new pair to replace them. Another store sold leather goods, suitcases, briefcases, wallets. I bought a medium-priced briefcase as well as pens and writing pads and put everything into it. That way, no matter where I went on the ship, I could take the diary along.

In one of the bars, to discourage conversation, I took out one of the pads and began to write in it, looking as preoccupied as I could. The bar had blond paneling, a soft carpet, a unobstrusive piano player, two bartenders, and three waiters. Most of the people at the bar and at the tables were Dutch, solid and prosperous, not quite as hearty as the few Germans and Americans in the place. I sat and drank Jack Daniel's and water and made an occasional note. A few people glanced at me, no doubt thinking I was a dull fellow to have along on a fun-filled cruise. The piano player played but didn't sing, and when he wasn't doing his own stuff he took requests, made mostly by the Germans, who liked that sort of thing. I was beginning to relax after all the tension I'd been through. Maybe it's going to be all right, I thought, ordering another Daniel's with a lot of water in it.

I got out of the bar when one of the Germans, slightly drunk, took over the piano and began to sing. His friends joined him, all singing out of key but plenty loud. I have an irrational dislike of German songs, and maybe it comes from all the young West Germans I've seen in Texas, where they're trained as pilots by the U.S. Air Force.

Whatever the reason, I went back to my cabin, called room service, ordered a steak and a baked potato. Then I drank beer and watched the ship's own television stations. They had three, at least in first class. One station was in Dutch, one in German, one in English. The last had syndicated programs, mostly sitcoms and game shows, from the States, nothing heavy, just garbage.

On a table were slick paper magazines from all over. I read *Time* and *Newsweek* until I got sick of them. Then it got dark and I went to sleep with the .45 under my pillow. Morning came and I still had the diary and nobody had tried to kill me.

The next day I went to a movie while the steward made up my cabin. I got some books from the ship's library, ate room service food, drank good Dutch beer, settled in for another day at sea. I was bored, but being dead was worse.

There were women on board that would have been worth a tumble at any other time. But for now, celibacy was the best policy; I figured to make up for it as soon as people stopped trying to kill me. On the ship it was fun and games from early morning till late at night. People played bridge, ping-pong, shuffleboard; they swam and sunned themselves and watched first-run movies. You got to know the ones that wanted to play musical beds. A lot of screwing goes on on cruise ships and more than one couple has gone on board holding hands and sailed back to a divorce.

I didn't mind it after I got used to it. The food was good and there was plenty of it. I drank enough, but never went to bed with a load on, because the job wasn't over yet and I had yet to drop my anchor in a safe harbor. But the more I considered my chances, the better they looked. After you've been bouncing around the world as long as I have, you get to know when people are giving you the once-over for the wrong reasons. As far as I knew, there had been none of that. People, especially unattached women, looked me over and decided what I was, or what I wasn't. A few put themselves in my way. I was able to get out of it without hurting anyone's feelings or otherwise drawing attention to myself.

I remember one old broad who scolded me for always wearing a jacket. "You're so formal, Mr. De Pauw," she said, twittering like a cracked canary. "Why don't you loosen up and get with it? I never see you at the pool and there are so many fun things to do. I'm surprised you don't take part in any of them."

How could I tell her that I wore a jacket to hide the forty-five? I carried the big Colt at all times; at night I slept with it under my pillow.

One day followed another. The days were no

sweat, but the nights were the best for me. Late at night, after the fun and games finally stopped, it was good to go up on deck and look at the sea and feel the wind and not have to talk to anybody.

We got to Zamboanga.

ELEVEN

I had to go on deck, then cross the deck, to get a look at it. Seen from the ship, it seemed different from the city I'd arrived in by plane such a short time before. Early in the morning, with the sun just up, Zamboanga appeared smaller, as if the entire city had been built along the water's edge. I saw the massive walls of Fort Pilar, built in the 17th century, according to the Dutch officer who was describing it to the passengers lined up along the rail, waiting for the launches that would take them ashore. He said the tall buildings, just a few, in the center of town were government offices and new hotels.

"Zamboanga was the scene of many fierce battles between the Spanish and the Moros," the Dutchman was saying, doing his best to make it sound interesting, "and the Spanish influence is still felt in the local dialect which has a heavy mixture of Spanish in it. Pasonanca Park is one of the loveliest in the country, and I'm sure you'll want to visit it. And for those of you interested in shell collection, I can assure you that Zamboanga is a shell collector's paradise. The city also has a Barter Trade Market for good buys in Muslim brassware, handwoven fabrics and batik. We'll be going ashore in a moment."

The first of the launches pulled away from the ship; I was more interested in what might be coming out. The *Wilhelmina* was anchored about a thousand yards out and I used my binoculars like the other passengers who had them. Customs men, a few uniformed police, stood around on the dock where the launches would tie up. No police boats came out and I relaxed a little. After the deck was clear I got a deck chair and sat in it, watching the town, but not doing it all the time. I got a steward to bring me a beer; two hours went by and nothing happened. Ten hours to go, I thought.

Launches came and went from the ship, and some of those who returned complained that Zamboanga was nothing to write home about. Still no police boats. If they were planning to search the ship, they were taking their time about it. But I couldn't be sure, so I stayed where I was.

We had anchored at six in the morning; now it was late afternoon, just after five, and I had seen nothing that made me think I wouldn't get to Manila. The steward, who asked me to call him Johnny because his name was Jan, brought me another beer and that morning's edition of the Manila *Times* flown in only a few hours before.

I looked at the front page and froze; Van Dalen's face, modestly smiling, gazed out at the world, and the story that went with the picture said he'd been tortured and then shot to death. Just like Mrs. Sanders. Here is how the story went:

DUTCH TRAVEL AGENT
VICTIM OF TORTURE MURDER

Davao. Mindanao. The mutilated body of Martin Van Dalen, 40, popular local representative of Netherlands Tours of Amsterdam, was discovered early yesterday in swampland close to the city. Police report Mr. Van Dalen had been tortured before being shot in the head.

"It appears Mr. Van Dalen was the victim of kidnappers who panicked before any ransom demands could be made," a Davao Police Constabulary spokesman said. "However, we are investigating all possibilities, and no stone will be left unturned until his murderers have been brought to justice."

Mr. Van Dalen, a bachelor, retired from the Amsterdam police detective division five years ago and took up his executive position in Davao shortly thereafter.

A member of the Davao Chamber of Commerce and an enthusiastic "booster" of Dutch-Philippine cultural and trade relations, Mr. Van Dalen will be missed by his many Filipino friends who are shocked and saddened by his slaying.

Funeral arrangements will be made after relatives in the Netherlands are located.

I folded the newspaper and went back to my cabin. A short newspaper story had changed my entire situation; there was a lot of rethinking to do. The secret police wanted me bad, but they hadn't killed Mrs. Sanders and they hadn't killed Van Dalen. If they'd killed him, and knew I was on the ship, it would have been boarded the moment it dropped anchor outside Zamboanga harbor. Like as not, a coastal patrol boat would have come out to make sure it didn't skip its port of call. I knew the Moros hadn't killed Mrs. Sanders, which made it fairly sure that they hadn't worked the same method on Van Dalen. Isolated in Mindanao, they just didn't have that kind of intelligence apparatus. So that left the Americans, the ones Van Dalen had been told about by Dutch Intelligence, that were responsible for the murders. It couldn't be anyone else. Van Dalen's body had been found early the day before, which seemed to indicate that he had been killed during the night and his body dumped under cover of darkness, and that gave them all the time they needed to get to Zamboanga before the cruise ship arrived. A car, a light plane, anything was faster than the leisurely speed of a vacation liner. They could, I thought, be on the boat right now.

I keep saying *they* because I didn't know what they looked like, or how many of them there were. Van Dalen called them thugs, but thugs don't always look like thugs. There might be a few goons with thick necks and bent noses in the outfit, brought along to handle the brute stuff; the men who told them what to do, far from looking like thugs, might be as mild-mannered as Mr. Whipple in the toilet paper commercials.

I locked the door and looked around the cabin. Nothing had been disturbed that I could see. Which meant nothing. Sometimes a pro snooper will go so far as to take Polaroids so he won't have to remember what a place looked like before he started his search. And these guys—who could doubt it?—were real professionals.

A big cruise ship is a floating city, except that everything is packed closer. But all the elements are there, from the magnificence of the captain's table to the brig, where an occasional criminal must be confined until he is landed over to the police at the next port of call. There are bars, laundries, shops, places of worship, movie theaters, libraries, a hospital. You can hide on a cruise ship if you know how to do it.

I had no hard evidence that they were on board; I just knew it. Several days sailing time lay between Zamboanga and Manila. They might make their move within hours, they might wait for the last night at sea. A knife, a silenced bullet, a knock on the head; a body made a small splash in that big sea. It was dark now and I could hear a band playing. Every night there was a dance going on somewhere.

The phone rang and I answered it.

"This is room service," a voice with a slight foreign accent said. "Did you just call, sir? There seems to be a mix-up here. Sorry to bother you. Just checking, sir."

"No, I didn't call you," I said.

"Thank you, Mr. De Pauw," the voice said. "I hope I haven't disturbed you."

I told him that was all right, and hung up. Then I called room service and got a voice I recognized.

"No sir," he said. "We haven't called you. We're very careful about things like that. We keep a log of all calls. It goes into a computer for billing purposes. Are you sure the caller mentioned room service?"

"Maybe I got it wrong. I'd been asleep. It isn't important."

"It's very important to us, sir." He sounded concerned, as if room service had been accused of not being on the ball. "Is there anything I can do for you?"

"No, thanks. I guess I was mistaken."

I hung up and waited with the .45 in my hand. We hadn't been at sea very long; already they were checking to make sure of where I was. There was no way off the ship, not in that shark-infested sea, and I couldn't go to the captain, because he'd throw me in the brig, then get on the radio to the Philippines police. I'd be safe enough in the brig, but that would last only as long as it took the police to send a patrol boat out to the ship. After that I wouldn't be safe at all, and asking to see a U.S. consul would get me laughed at. In the end, I'd just wind up dead.

There was nothing to do but go out and face them. Don't ask me how. I didn't know their faces; there were so many faces on the ship. But anything was better than being cooped up waiting for something to happen. What I had to do, for openers, was to put the diary where they couldn't just walk in and take it. The purser's safe, or strongroom, had plenty of valuable stuff in it, mostly jewelry, and it would be well guarded. I decided to give it a try.

The night man was on duty and he showed no surprise when I said I wanted to hand over the airline bag for safekeeping. Cruise ships get their share of eccentrics, and maybe he thought there was a gold bar in it. He took the bag and an armed sailor sitting inside a recessed cage opened the door and locked it after him. Then the purser gave me a receipt and I went to the bar with the blond wood paneling.

There were no unoccupied tables, so I sat at the end of the bar and ordered a beer. I saw the woman with the copper-streaked hair being glamorous at one of the tables. The guy she was with, a burly man about fifty, was hanging onto her every word. None of the community-sing Germans was there.

When you're being hunted, you look at faces and wonder which one means to kill you. The ones that look most likely hardly ever are. Just because a guy has shifty eyes and a bulge in his pocket doesn't mean he's an assassin with a too obvious gun. That bulge may be nothing more lethal than a transistor radio or a ham sandwich.

A man sitting beside me tried to strike up a conversation, and I let him. He sounded like a New Englander or someone who had gone to school there. Early forties, thin brown hair that might have been dyed, cord suit, button-down oxford shirt, striped tie. A vacationing professor? A magazine writer? A hired killer? No way to tell.

"Haven't seen you on board," he said. "My name is Blake."

"De Pauw," I said. "I came aboard at Davao. I'd seen enough of the islands. There was a vacancy. Somebody had to go to the hospital at Cape Town."

"Ah yes, that would be old Mr. Peters. I think he was some kind of academic. A pity, having his trip cut short like that."

Blake said he was taking the cruise for his health. "I'm in town planning in Hartford. Just been through a nasty divorce and it got me a bit rattled. My doctor advised me to get away from it all. Expensive, though, but I suppose this will be my first and last cruise. I don't know about you, I find it sort of dull."

"It can be," I agreed.

I told him the yarn Van Dalen had prepared for me. It was as good as any other. After fifteen years in the army I had come into an inheritance from a Texas bachelor uncle. Now, six months later, I was still undecided about what I wanted to do.

"You want my advice?" Blake said. "About how to handle your money?"

A con man, I thought, but I was wrong.

"Don't do anything," he said. "Put your money in the bank and live off the interest. Investments can be a headache. All my life I worked to put away a little nest egg and look at me. Nervous as a cat. Enjoy life, Mr. De Pauw. That's what it's there for."

I could see that he wanted to talk about himself. The story of his dull life unfolded like a featureless road with nothing but NO EXIT signs on it. He was drinking scotch and water, but his self-pity was more intoxicating than the booze. I didn't mind too much; all I had to do was nod and grunt once in a while. People came in and went out. A different piano player was there, a middle-aged fag with a worn face who ran his fingers over brittle cocktail music.

Blake was telling me about the professional jealousy he had to contend with in his job. "I know town planning sounds dull, but it can be quite exciting. Like life, it depends on what you put into it."

"Uh-huh," I said.

A guy seemed to be studying me in the bar mirror. He was by himself, a few stools down, with a tall drink in front of him, tapping the side of his glass with a swizzle stick, keeping time to the music. Tall and thin, any age between forty and fifty. He looked familiar, or maybe it was just his type. He was the kind that got things done. Middle management, highly efficient. I was just guessing, but there are times when you have to trust past experience and hope you're right.

"You probably don't agree with me," Blake was saying.

"Not completely," I said. A safe thing to say, it covers a lot of ground.

"Well, it happens to be the truth," Blake went on. "Low cost housing has been a failure in this country. I know that from bitter, hard-won experience. Instant slums, that's what these projects are. A better solution must be found for the problems of the inner city. Take that St. Louis housing development of not so many years ago. They tried everything to make it work. Finally, someone suggested dynamiting the damned thing. That's what they did. Sensible but horribly wasteful, millions of dollars down the drain. Surely you remember, or were you overseas at the time?"

"I read about it," I said.

Blake finished his drink and began to look less than steady. "Oops!" he said. "I think it's time for beddy-bye. Hope to have another chat real soon. De Pauw, that's the name, isn't it?"

I said it was, and after he left I got another beer and waited for something to happen. It took a while. It was getting late and the bar crowd thinned out, and as soon as there was a table available the stranger took it. A waiter carried the stranger's drink, then came back to me.

"Gentleman over there thinks you have mutual friends and would you care to join him for a drink? This is his card." The waiter kept his face deadpan; what went on between consenting adults was no business of his.

The card gave the stranger's name as William Paterson, his address was 137 O'Farrell Street, San Francisco. No business was given. I turned and he was watching for my reaction; a polite smile told me I was welcome to join him if I felt like it.

I took my beer to the table. "The waiter says you think you know me. Where would that be from?"

"From General Sanders' diary," he said, adding quickly, "and there's no cause for violence. I'd like to talk, all right?"

I sat down. "Talk costs nothing, so talk."

"Sometimes a talk can be very profitable. But I won't beat around the bush. I know you have the diary. How much do you want for it?"

"It's not for sale."

"Everything is for sale. For instance, how much is your life worth to you?"

"That's not for sale either."

"So you say. Look at it this way. You're many miles out at sea. You can run but you can't hide. Joe Louis. You can't even run. You can't call for the police. I know you're armed, but so are we. You know what I look like, but not my friends. We'll kill you if we have to—make no mistake about that—but where's the profit? If we were on land you wouldn't be given a choice. Out here, it's different. We could probably put you over the side and let the sharks have you. Why risk it?"

"Then don't do it."

"We'd prefer not to," Paterson said.

"Did you kill Van Dalen and Mrs. Sanders?"

"Yes. I want you to know how serious we are. Look here, you have a great gift for survival, but it can't last indefinitely. Give it up, take the money, and that's the end of it. Case closed."

"How much money?"

"I'm authorized to pay you fifty thousand dollars in cash. None of it counterfeit. I'm sure you can tell real money from queer."

"Fifty thousand doesn't sound like much."

"Fifty thousand and a bonus, your life. It's well worth considering."

"I've already got my life," I said.

"But not for long," Paterson said.

"How would it work if I agreed?"

Paterson sipped at his tall drink. "We know you gave the diary to the purser. A wise move you might have made sooner. Don't deny it, you were seen. Get the diary back, I'll hand over the money, and we'll be gone from your life."

"Gone how? It's still a long way to Manila."

"A boat will take us off shortly after you give us the diary. Arrangements have been made. Money talks. I hope it talks to you. If you have any doubts, you can wave to us as we take off. I don't know what can be fairer than that. Don't fight it, Rainey. You've given us a good run, but now it's over and you have no place to go."

"You aren't afraid I might talk later?"

"Talk about what? There's no proof—you can't have Xeroxed the diary in the jungle. No one will listen to you. Any sensible person would regard you as a publicity-seeker or a crank. Talk if you feel like talking, although you'd be a fool if you did. Now what's it going to be?"

"No deal," I said. Paterson might have the diary and leave the ship, but there would be someone left on board to get rid of me.

"Seventy-five thousand?" Paterson said.

I shook my head. I'll take my chances.

"One hundred thousand?"

"No deal."

Paterson got up and went out without another word. There was no head shaking, no sighs or exasperation of regret. Our talk had been nothing more than an exercise, a way of sounding me out. Now he knew, and so did I.

What Paterson would do next could only be guessed at. There would be a meeting with his associates. He spoke of them in the plural; there might not be more than one. The meeting would decide how they were going to deal with me. True, I was confined to the ship, but so were they, at least for the moment. Killing a man is easy enough; it's getting rid of the body that makes it messy, and a cruise ship never settled down completely. Lovers taking a turn on the deck in the moonlight, a playful drunk passed out in a lifeboat, an insomniac gazing at the sea. The kind of chance that Paterson couldn't afford. No, they might not come at me tonight, but they'd be along just the same.

I got on the phone in the bar and asked for Mr. Paterson's cabin number. The operator said no such person was on the passenger list. But there was a Mr. Parsons and perhaps I had the names confused.

I thanked her and hung up. It didn't matter. It was no big maneuver on Paterson's part. He just didn't want to be surprised in his cabin.

I wondered how he planned to get the diary away from the purser's care. A stick-up would be dumb unless he wrecked the ship's radio system and had a chopper waiting to take him off. That would be one way of doing it, yet it wasn't his style as I had come to see it.

I left the bar and went to the dance for the passengers. Like the bar, it had thinned out, but there were enough die-hards left to give me some protection.

It was a dance without too much disco, which can be rough on middle-aged hearts. The music was brassy and bland at the same time. This was what cruise ship musicians call The Corset Crowd, and many of the revelers were of an age where they still preferred gin to vodka drinks. The women were in better shape than the men. Now and then streamers and balloons floated down from the ceiling. Behind the service bar, rows of empty champagne bottles stood in their cases. Paterson wasn't on the dance floor or on the sidelines.

The dance wasn't going to last much longer. Even now, all but the most energetic dancers were starting to look tired. There is nothing more tiring than having a good time. A woman with too many face lifts asked me to dance and I went out on the floor with her. She was one of those dancers that know how good they are and like to show off. I was only fair to middling and she begged off in the middle of the dance, saying she thought a strap on her shoe was coming undone. I think we'd been doing a rumba, but maybe it was a samba. That's the kind of dancer I am. Her shoe must have been self repairing, because she was back on the floor within minutes. This time her partner was a youngish guy with false hair woven into his own thinning locks. I guess it was better than a toupee, which I'm told are sometimes snatched off in moments of passion. They were very good together and got some envious glances, and if they learned what they did at Arthur Murray, then the money hadn't been wasted.

It was getting late and I still had no plan of action, and locking myself in my cabin was no way to handle the situation; they can always get at you if you don't have the right defenses.

The band played on: disco for the agile, more stately music for the corset crowd. I got a drink at the bar and stayed there. A guy was telling another guy how much he liked to disco but couldn't because he had a bad back. The other guy winked and said, "I trust you suffered it in the line of duty." That got a laugh and the first guy told a story about a roller derby queen he shacked up with in Kansas City. To judge by his winks and pauses it was a story he had told many times before. He looked like a supporting player who used to play young, wisecracking GI's in 1940's war movies. Now he was old enough to play retired generals.

"Actually, it didn't happen in bed," he said. "She was a regular little hell-raiser, but I gave as good as I got. What happened was, I stepped on one of her skates when I tried to rush off to catch my flight to Chicago. Zip! Crash! Down I went on the flat of my back. I lay there groaning and you know what she said, the sexy little bitch? Should I call a chiropractor or what? she said, and even with the pain I had to laugh. You know, there isn't a time I get a pain in my back I don't think of that little devil. A non-stop sex machine was what she was. You've heard of someone having a motor mouth? Well sir, this little doll had a motor pussy."

"I envy you," the other man said.

I moved away from the dirty old men, still trying to decide what to do. As happens so often, the decision was made for me.

TWELVE

A firebell cut loose, drowning out the mellow sounds of the orchestra. The orchestra stopped playing and the leader got on the microphone and urged the partygoers not to panic. He was still urging calm and cooperation when his mike went dead and the captain took over on the general public address system. The captain was as calm as a deacon.

"A fire has broken out, but will be shortly under control. You will see smoke and men with fire-fighting equipment, but there is no cause for alarm. I repeat, there is a fire in progress, but you need not worry. All my men have been trained for emergencies of this kind. Stay where you are. Stay where you are. Wait for the instructions of the ship's officers. There is no immediate danger."

The captain went off the air and the band began to play. They did that on the *Titanic* after it ran into the iceberg. God didn't listen. The woman who was showing off got back on the floor with a different partner. Her friend with the woven hair was at the bar gulping down a double. A florid-faced drunk applauded the exhibitionist's courage, tried to find his own partner, was turned down. So he danced by himself, making elaborate dips and bows. He wasn't afraid because he was so drunk. Most of the others were afraid and showing it or not showing it in different ways. There are few things as bad as a fire at sea. All too often the lifeboats burn like matchwood and even when they're not made of wood something goes wrong with them. Fire drills are supposed to help. They do help, but they'd help a lot more if the passengers took them seriously. No smoke was coming under the door. So far it wasn't that dramatic.

The captain cut in on the orchestra, but wasn't too specific about the progress being made. I disobeyed his order to stay put and went to take a look. Other people were wandering about looking for reassurance. Some had the dazed look that comes with being tumbled out of bed without any clear idea of what's happening. Ship's officers, not so dapper now, were doing their best to prevent a panic.

I grabbed one of the stewards and wouldn't let go till he told me what was happening. "A fire. What do you think, sir? A fire?" He looked ready to go over the side.

I shook him hard. "I know there's a fire. Where is it?"

He was no seaman, just a seagoing waiter. "There's several fires. I don't know how bad they are. Let me go, sir."

I turned him loose and he darted up a companionway. Paterson, I thought. The son of a bitch had set fires—had them set—as a cover for knocking over the purser's cage. I went up on deck and saw smoke coming from a ventilator. No flame yet, but plenty of smoke. The smoke smelled like burning celluloid and that can be as bad as tear gas. I bumped into the dancing drunk from the ballroom. He got in my way. I stepped to one side. He stepped the same way. I shoved him into a deck chair and he lay there, laughing.

The purser's office and strongroom were located amidships, and lung-searing smoke billowed from that direction. It was a nightmarish scene, the great white ship moving smoothly through a glassy sea, trailing oily black smoke. A ship's officer, not the captain, probably the first mate, was talking on the PA system. People turned their faces toward the speakers, but I'm not sure they understood what he was saying. Panic is like that.

Fighting my way through the mob on deck, I finally reached the purser's office. The door was closed but not locked. I went in and closed it behind me. My eyes jumped to the steel door to the strongroom. It was open and the purser and the guard lay together with their mouths taped, their hands cuffed behind them. Lockbox 30 was open and the diary was gone.

I couldn't find a key to the handcuffs, but I removed the tape from their mouths. The purser was conscious and red-faced with indignation. Beside him the guard lay with his eyes rolled back. His breathing was weak and shallow. Concussion, maybe a skull fracture. I helped the purser to his feet and steadied him.

"There are fires all over the ship," I said. "I

don't think it's serious, but it looks bad. Are you all right?"

He nodded.

"Then go get help for the guard. I'm going to look for the men who started the fires. Did you see them? How many?"

"Two men." Quickly he described Paterson. "The other man was shorter and heavier. Both had pistols. What are they to you, sir? What did they steal from you?"

"Never mind that. Get help for the guard." I pushed him toward the door. "There must be bolt cutters on board. They'll get the handcuffs off. If you have to take to the boats, you can't do it with your hands behind your back."

I followed him out. He disappeared into the smoke, coughing hard, unable to cover his mouth. Looking for Paterson was a hopeless job, and if I found him at all it would be by accident. The captain was back on the sound system, still telling the passengers not to panic, there was no danger, but just the same he was putting in as close to the shore as he would manage without endangering the ship.

"We are getting the fire under control," he repeated. "A most unfortunate accident. Do not panic. Damage has been minor and there have been no injuries."

The smoke did seem to be lessening, but the passengers remained in a state close to total panic. A woman screamed, "We're all going to die!" until another woman slapped her, warning her to shut up. I thought I heard a boat, but couldn't be sure because of the uproar. At the rail, trying to listen, I heard it again. It was a powerful boat. I could tell by the deep rumble of the engine. It was coming through the smoke that drifted down from the ship and hung over the water. Other people heard it and began to call out, begging to be taken off. The boat moved along the side of the ship; somebody was talking through a bullhorn. The voice was shouting, "Let it down, then come down after it."

I ran toward the sound of the horn. My eyes were hot and red, my lungs felt as if they were on fire. A gust of wind blew some of the smoke away and I saw Paterson and another man readying a rope to go over the side. Paterson had a pistol in his hand and he fired at me and missed. The other man was carrying my airline bag. He turned and fired too. I fired back and killed him. Paterson, calm as if he'd been on a target range, held his pistol in both hands and returned my fire. On a target range, his shooting would have been great; on a ship with a slight roll, all his shots went wild. He tried to toss the diary over the side, but the roll of the ship beat him again. The bag hit the rail and bounced back on the deck. I shot Paterson in the head while he was bending to grab it up. One bullet was enough. Bits of gray-white bone flew away from his skull and he went down hard. I was moving in to check the bodies when Dutchmen came at me from behind. Only a few had revolvers. A few was enough. I heard the motor boat roaring away from the ship.

"Now then," the captain said with Dutch stolidity, "what is this business all about? Who are you and why did you kill these two men? Who are they?"

The purser whispered to the captain. "I see,"

the captain said. "Van Dalen."

The purser whispered again. "I see," the captain said again, looking at the airline bag on the deck beside the dead men.

The second officer was just about to pick up the bag when the man who called himself Blake came forward through the drifting smoke.

"Leave it where it is," he ordered. "I'll take it."

The captain eyed him. "What's it got to do with you?"

The smoke was blowing away fast and the ship's junior officers were holding back the more daring passengers. It wasn't every day you saw two dead men on the deck of a cruise ship.

"A security matter," Blake said, adding, "Dutch security."

This so-called town planner reached into his pocket and showed the captain his credentials. The captain studied them carefully. "I must radio about this," he said.

"There's a number on there," Blake said. "That's all you'll need."

Two crewmen had covered the body. Behind us passengers were asking questions. One was asking if the dead men had been bandits come aboard to steal the jewels in the purser's strongroom.

"I must radio about this," the captain repeated, as if the words had some magic quality. He was a youngish man with white hair, and though not yet fifty, he had a stiff, elderly manner. A competent man, but self-important.

"Then radio, sir," Blake said.

"This man was put aboard this ship by our

man in Davao. Van Dalen." The captain looked at me with immense suspicion. "Since then Van Dalen has been murdered. Did you know that?"

Blake remained unperturbed. "I did, Captain. Then he couldn't have done it, could he? Please radio. But not the Philippine police. This is a Dutch ship."

"These men were killed in Philippine waters. But all right. I'll radio, but I won't be responsible for anything. You are not in the clear, either." He turned to the two officers holding revolvers. "Take these two men below and watch them. You"—he pointed to a junior officer—"have the bodies removed to the hospital. I'll radio, all right. Damned right I will! I must have authority before I do anything else."

The two officers marched us down to a remote cell with two bunks, a very clean toilet and sink, and air-conditioning. Blake sat on a bunk with the airline bag beside him.

"This shouldn't take long," he said confidently.

"Who the hell are you? Are you really Dutch intelligence?"

"Jacob Nagel. And I *am* Dutch intelligence."

"You sure as hell don't sound Dutch."

"We have a good training school."

"Can you prove all this?"

He showed his ID, with photograph, thumbprint, signature. The card had been embossed with a crown and the number he'd given the captain was there.

The air-conditioner hummed. It was too cold in there. "You can buy a card like that for a thousand dollars," I said.

He took the card back and tapped it. "Not a number like this one. The card perhaps, not the number. Not for ten thousand dollars. Much more than that. When the captain gets through, they'll ask him for the number, then they'll feed it into a computer. That'll verify my identity."

"Okay," I said. "Suppose they can. But how did you get onto me, and why the favor? It's a big favor, but what's it got to do with Dutch intelligence?"

Nagel shivered in the blast of the air conditioning. "They can't use this place too much," he said. "Van Dalen used to do some freelance work for us. Small stuff. Passed on tips, etcetera. A crook in a small way, but useful, so when he asked us to check you out, we did. That's when rumors of this diary turned up. Did Van Dalen tell you we told him about it?"

"He did."

"He lied. We'd never do that. He got word from somewhere else, probably the secret police. A tricky fellow, Mr. Van Dalen. Anyway, we'd heard about it because a lot of blackmailers were buzzing about it. So we called our American counterparts—professional curiosity and professional courtesy—and they hedged, of course. We all do in our trade."

"Did you ask the Americans about me?"

Nagel smiled. "Not that I can remember. Anyway, we decided there must be something to the whole business. I knew Van Dalen fairly well, which meant I knew there must be money involved. His shady dealings were of no interest to us, naturally, but if the Americans were involved, then it was quite another matter."

"Why? You haven't answered my question.

Why was your service so interested?"

Another tricky smile. "Intelligence people are interested in everything that goes on. Part of the game. Knowledge is power, as they say. So I went to Davao to take a look for myself. Van Dalen had gone to glory by the time I got there. The girl at his office told me about you and this ship. She was too frightened not to. I flew to Zamboanga and got aboard. I have a Dutch passport. No problem at all."

I looked at this glib character. "Van Dalen said you couldn't get on a cruise ship after it had sailed from its port of origin. You couldn't have used your Intelligence ID to get on board or they'd know about you."

"I wish the captain would hurry up," Nagel said. "Van Dalen was a liar. I've told you that. He probably wanted you to think it was so difficult to get you on the ship. More money, naturally."

"Naturally. Then you knew these guys were after me?"

"I knew somebody was after you. You did business with Van Dalen and right after that he wasn't just murdered, but tortured. Naturally the girl at the office didn't know why. How could she? They wouldn't have bothered her after they got all they wanted from Van Dalen."

"Hard world, isn't it?" I said.

"Yeah." Nagel sounded very American. "Too many bad people in it."

Footsteps came down the hall. They sounded hollow on the steel plates. The door was unlocked and there was only one young officer this time. He wasn't holding a gun. He even grinned. He spoke to Nagel in Dutch.

"It's all right," Nagel said to me. "But the captain wants to see us in his cabin. He's very worried."

I could see the captain's point. A middle-aged guy is running a nice respectable cruise ship and three other guys have a gun battle on the deck and two of them wind up dead.

"Come along, gentlemen," the young officer said.

The captain was behind his desk, looking worried. His beautiful white hair was mussed as if he'd been running his fingers through it. "Lock the door," he said to Nagel.

We sat down.

"Well?" Nagel said.

The captain sighed. "Yes, there's no doubt you work for our intelligence service. Amsterdam told me very little. But very well, you have the authority to prevent this man's arrest. On this ship, anyway. But he must leave the ship at Manila."

"Please explain."

"I didn't just talk to your people, I talked to mine. A compromise has been reached."

"Why can't he go on to Australia?"

"No! No!" The captain gave the desk a thump. "That isn't what's wanted. He killed two men and we can't just throw the bodies over the side. The matter has to be reported in Manila. Our government doesn't want to risk any incident with the Filipinos. He must get off this ship as soon as we dock. Escape. Run away. They'll complain about that, but this is a cruise ship, not a prison ship. We'll say he broke out, that's all. But it must be reported to the authorities. There were too many witnesses to cover it up."

Nagel frowned. "You don't know what the Philippine police are like. They'll hunt him down like a dog."

"Not if he's quick. Let him go to the American embassy."

Nagel turned to me. "You want to try that?"

"It's better than the police. You'll have to tell me where it is. I don't know the city."

Nagel said, "I'll make a map for you. But I can't go with you. The secret police know who I am. You think the embassy will protect you? You're hardly a political fugitive."

I pointed to the bag. "Maybe I have something to bargain with."

Nagel rubbed his chin. "A little political blackmail. It might work if they give you a hard time."

The captain said quickly, "I don't want to hear any of this. Now I'm a very busy man, if you don't mind. Mr. De Pauw, or whatever your name is, you'll have to go back in the brig until it's time to let you go. I don't want the passengers to see you and become upset. You may have anything you want from room service— within reason, that is. Your departure will be arranged on the night of our arrival. Not by me. I hope never to see you again. Goodbye."

The young officer was called and told to take me to jail. Nagel came along to visit. I ordered beer and ham sandwiches and magazines. The young officer came back in less than ten minutes. Room service was pretty good on the *Wilhelmina*.

"I'll be standing guard," the young Dutchman said. "The door has to be locked when Mr. Nagel leaves. Captain's orders."

I opened a bottle of beer. "In a few minutes," I said.

"Yes, sir," he said.

I looked at the steel door with the little barred slot. "You sure the captain won't change his mind and radio the police? I'd rather go over the side in a rubber boat than have that happen."

Nagel was drinking one of the beers. "I think it'll be okay. He knows what he has to do. He just doesn't want to do it. There's a difference."

"I hope so." I listened to the smooth throb of the ship. The brig seemed like a steel coffin. "Can a ship as big as this dock right in Manila harbor?"

"Any time. I've seen this one there often. Comes right into the city. All you have to do is get off and walk to the embassy. It isn't far." He put the airline bag on the bed. "You've come a long way with this thing, haven't you?"

"Maybe too far."

"Then why did you do it?"

"Because I'm stubborn."

"Maybe too stubborn."

"Water over the dam, Nagel."

"See you in the morning, Rainey. I've had enough of this place—sorry I said that."

I was sorry too, after he'd gone and the door was locked. Up on deck there would be wind and sky, and in the bar, drinks and music. The bag with the diary in it lay on the other bunk. I was finally in a place I couldn't just walk out of and I didn't like the feeling. Everyone is afraid of something.

I drank the rest of the beer and read the magazines. If I get out of this, I thought, the next job I take will be fighting in some nice simple little war.

The beer put me to sleep.

In the morning, Nagel came with the map. It showed where the ship would dock, where the American embassy was. A simple map. Like he said, all I had to do was walk away. Yeah.

We went over the map again. Nagel insisted on it. "We'll be docking here," he said, pointing. "That's the Tondo, right behind the harbor, and it's the worst and most dangerous slum in Manila. You'll have to go through it if you want to stay off the main streets. Just don't get yourself murdered after all you've been through. Keep that forty-five ready, but try not to shoot it off."

I grinned at him. "Not unless I have to. Don't teach me my business."

"I wouldn't think of it."

"The only thing you haven't told me is how I get off the ship."

"As a crew member. After the visitors have gone, the few that go at night. Most of them will wait till morning. Dangerous foreign city, you know. I have clothes and seaman's papers fixed up for you. Just wave the papers at the police or immigration if they look at you. They probably won't. Nobody looks at a sailor off a ship."

"Let's hope."

"It's the best I can do for you."

"It's pretty good."

"Remember, you walk. No taxis. Half the taxi drivers there are police spies."

207

"I told you, don't teach me my business. How is the captain taking all this?"

"He doesn't know a thing about it. Officially. You want to look at the map again?"

"No, it's inscribed on my brain, like they say. One more time—you still say you're doing all this for Dutch intelligence?"

"That's the first reason."

"And the second?"

Nagel looked embarrassed. It didn't go with the rest of him. In his pose as Blake, the town planner from Hartford, it would have gone fine.

"A spook from Texas once saved my life."

"I like that reason better," I said.

THIRTEEN

The docks blazed with light and the passengers, mostly men, who wanted to see some nightlife, had already gone ashore. I had waited in the shadow of the bridge long enough. Now it was time to go.

It was quiet now except for the sounds of the ship. I couldn't see the men at the bottom of the gangplank. Their Filipino voices were faint at that distance. Beyond the docks, in the Rondo, the streets had more darkness than light. That's where I was going.

I was heading for the gangplanks when two seamen came up on deck and down ahead of me. The cops didn't ask to see their papers. I went down carrying the airline bag. The .45 was in my pants pocket with the slide snapped and the safety on.

It was a long gangplank because it was that big a ship. I felt as naked as a stripper on an old burlesque runway. Because this was a cruise ship, the cops didn't have submachine guns. But they had pistols, and pistols would be enough. There were immigration men with the cops. I didn't know if they had pistols too. Most Filipino men like to carry big caliber automatics, nickel-plated if they can afford it.

They looked at me. I didn't do a thing but walk past and they didn't stop me. I had seaman's papers, but they might have my description. One would cancel out the other. They might have orders to take me alive, but Marcos' cops get carried away with their work.

Nothing happened.

I got a distance away from the lights and whores called me dirty names because I wouldn't stop. No sweat there: just as long as their pimps didn't try to stop me. The pimps, evil little bastards, let me pass. Maybe I was too big or the cops were too close. I had Nagel's map in my head and I was on a true course.

I had to cross the foul-smelling Passig River to get to Roxas Boulevard. That was where the American embassy was. Over there the lights were bright, the people well-dressed, but there was danger of another kind. In the Tondo, cops were few. Here, they were many.

Roxas Boulevard was the richest part of the city. On one side was Manila Bay. I could smell it, but I hadn't seen it yet. I'd been in the brig of the *Wilhelmina* when we came up from the south. On the other side of the boulevard were the hotels where the rich people stay. Nagel had mentioned the Hilton as a landmark in case I got lost. I guess he had a bad opinion of my sense of direction: Roxas Boulevard ran straight and wide for several miles. The embassy, according to the map, was about a mile from where I was now.

Traffic was heavier than in New York and not as well handled. Rich Filipinos don't like to be annoyed by traffic laws or traffic cops. In places, traffic was backed up for half a mile. Nobody seemed to mind too much. A traffic jam is one of the best ways to show off the new Mercedes. I was glad not to be driving. My sailor clothes didn't exactly suit this part of town, but nobody spat at me. I passed some uniformed city police. They took no notice of me. Another half mile and I'd be home free. They might not hug me like a brother, but I didn't think they'd throw me to the wolves.

The diary? Well, I suddenly wanted nothing more to do with the damned thing. I had hung onto it, come hell or high water, and now I didn't want it. The embassy could have it. I didn't care what they did with it. Publish it. Sell it, Suppress it. Use it for political blackmail. There would be a lot of questions and maybe I'd give truthful answers to some of them. Anything to get clear of this mess I was in.

The traffic moved about a hundred yards, then backed up again. A lot of quiet engines and loud stereos. I saw the lofty glitter of the Hilton, set back from the boulevard, and knew I didn't have far to go. I wondered what kind of interrogator I'd draw at the embassy. Every major embassy has a CIA agent posing as an attache as part of it. That's what I'd draw, I decided. A spook with a striped tie and over-the-calf socks. The ambassador would get a report, but I'd never get to see him. I wondered how they'd get me out if the Filipinos learned I was there. A diplomatic pouch, maybe.

I was walking past the next traffic back-up

when I saw a hard-faced Filipino looking at me from the window of a polished black Buick. A tough character more Spanish than Filipino, as a lot of them are. As I passed, he turned to speak to the driver. I walked on. I could see the bulk of the embassy about four hundred yards in the distance. Maybe they hadn't spotted me after all. But I knew they had.

Still walking, not fast, not slow, I expected to hear shouts and maybe running feet. Instead I heard a siren. It rose up to a howl and still nobody chased me on foot. They might be just suspicious and want to look me over. Maybe that was why there was no hot pursuit. I did the sensible thing: I started to run.

It was then that I heard car doors slamming. Next came the shouts and the running feet. The shouts, in English, were telling me to stop or they'd shoot. I ran faster with the .45 in my hand so I wouldn't lose it. Bullets came close, but I didn't turn and return fire. I would when they were right up on top of me. A bullet hit the bag and nearly tore it out of my hand. More bullets came, a whole hail of them. I just hung onto the .45 and kept running. Embassy or no embassy, I knew I'd never get out of Manila if I killed one of these bastards. Then a bullet ripped the heel off my shoe and I went down on my face. By the time I scrambled up, they were closing the distance. A minute later I ran through an open gate guarded by two Marines with M-16's.

"Where the fuck are you going, sir?" one of them yelled at me and brought up the M-16.

"I'm an American," I yelled back. "Two guys are trying to kill me!"

The other Marine, a monster of a guy,

brought me down in a flying tackle. "Hold on there, sir," he said. The first Marine pointed the M-16 at the gate. My secret police buddies were brought up short, their .45's in their hands.

The guy who had a grip on me was a sergeant, big as a barn, strong as a bull. "Stay behind me, sir," he ordered. "We'll have this squared away in a minute." He picked up his M-16 and said to the two Filipinos, "That you doin' all that shooting? You tryin' to kill this guy or somethin'? Ought to be more careful of guns, mister."

The two Filipinos looked at the automatic rifles. They didn't like it and the one who'd seen me first said in good English, "We are police and that man in there is under arrest. Send him out or there will be trouble."

"What's he done, officer?" the big sergeant said.

"Murder. Robbery. Illegal possession of weapons." The tough Filipino was so mad he wanted to shoot somebody, anybody. But in the face of the M-16's he thought better of it. He got legal again. "We have a warrant for his arrest. It is a very serious matter. I am ordering you to send him out. You have no right to keep him here. You are a foreigner in this country."

"You bet I am," the big sergeant said. "Fact is, I can't wait to get out of it."

"So you don't like our country? I don't like *your* stupid country! Are you so stupid that you don't know how serious this is? I demand to speak to someone in authority!"

The big sergeant just lifted the M-16. *"I'm* in authority," he said. "Now why don't you do what you do in the Corps? Go through channels. If you don't want to do that, then fuck off, Jack. Come through this gate and you'll go out in a body bag. I don't give a shit who you are, I ain't kiddin'."

The two Filipinos turned and walked away.

"Now sir," the big sergeant said calmly. "I think you're the one ought to speak to somebody in authority. That would be Mr. Mallory. First, though, I'll take that weapon you're carrying."

I gave it to him.

"What's in the bag?"

"Just a book, Sergeant."

"Let's take a look."

He let me keep the diary after he got his look.

I didn't get to see Mallory right away. The sergeant took me to a basement apartment of the no frills kind, gave me coffee and a sandwich, and told me to stay put till further notice. That was the sort of command I liked to hear.

I was watching Manila TV late that night when Mallory came in, a sour man without a striped tie. He wasn't CIA, I was certain. But you know how many intelligence agencies there are.

"Oh yes, we've been hearing about you," he said. "You've been causing more trouble than you're worth. We've been on the track of that diary for some time. You shouldn't have come here at all. You're a pain in the ass. You want protection now that you're in a mess, have the secret police after you. You don't deserve protection."

"I'm an American citizen," I said piously.

"Now you wave the flag. You wouldn't need

214

protection if you'd stayed in Texas."

I grinned at him. "You used to be a cop, didn't you?"

"None of your business."

"What are you now, Mallory?"

"Still none of your business."

I didn't see Mallory much except when he asked me questions. Mostly he wanted to hear about the Moros. I told him what I knew. The regional command, the rest of it. He got it all down on tape. I think he genuinely disliked me. I didn't think he was so bad.

The Filipinos made an awful stink at first. Mallory came through for me in the end. I knew it wasn't really up to him. He worked hard at it just the same. It was of no interest to me who fixed it. It was good to goof off without being shot at. Naturally I couldn't leave the embassy. I didn't want to. I drank beer and played poker with the Marines. All the intellectual things.

Then one day Mallory called me up to his office.

He said, "It hasn't been easy, squaring this with the police. I couldn't have done it by myself. It had to be fixed at the highest level. You don't look too grateful."

I shrugged. "How does a person look grateful? You want me to cry and kiss your hand?"

"You can kiss my ass, Rainey. I don't like you and don't you take me for a gruff cop with a heart of gold. Guys like you give me a pain. Ordinary soldiers risk their lives for a few hundred dollars a month. Wiseguys like you get rich."

"I didn't get rich on this one. What happens to the diary?"

Mallory didn't like to be questioned. "That's not for me to decide. It will probably be classified and kept out of bounds for maybe fifty years. That's what usually happens. It's none of your business what happens to it. I'm telling you to put it out of your mind."

"That's not so easy to do."

"Try hard. You never came to the islands, you never saw any diary. It's all a figment of your warped mind."

"I could forget the diary a lot easier if I knew more about it. As it is, I'm eaten up with curiosity. That keeps it foremost in my thoughts."

Mallory placed his hand on the battered cover of the diary, a possessive gesture, as if he half expected me to grab it away from him. His face was thin and tired.

"What else is there to know?" he said irritably. "You've read it, haven't you?"

"Sure I've read it. I've read it three times. I can understand why the men named in it would want it destroyed. I can even understand why one or two of them might hire killers to get that done. My question here is, why is army intelligence so concerned?"

"That's none of your business."

"Like hell it isn't. Come on, Mallory, who hired Paterson and his men to kill Van Dalen and Mrs. Sanders? Who is—was—Paterson?"

"We still can't be sure," Mallory said. I'm sure he was a good liar most of the time. Now he was tired and his heart wasn't in it.

"That's bullshit. You know or have a fair idea. Tell me or I may not be so cooperative. I might even go to the newspapers."

Mallory's eyes became dangerous. "That wouldn't be so smart."

"What'll you do? Put me on a ship to nowhere like Philip Nolan? Make me a new man without a country?"

"Always the wiseguy. Can't help it, I guess. I told you what I know."

"I want to know who Paterson was. I want to know who hired him. If you can trust me not to talk about the diary, then you can trust me with the rest of it."

"Hah! A minute ago you were running to the newspapers. Now you want to be trusted."

"I wouldn't go to the newspapers," I said. "Just trying on a bluff for size. You know I wouldn't want to get on the bad side of the government. Let's hear it, Mallory."

Mallory rubbed his face. "Jesus Christ, you'd think a guy like you would be glad to get out of the hole you got yourself into. But all right. A certain Southern California politician died of a stroke last week—a retired general turned businessman. Very high in GOP circles. I'm not sure he would ever have been brought to trial, but if he had the charge would have been conspiracy to commit murder. Now he's dead so it doesn't matter one way or another."

"You're talking about General Parsons? Parsons was right at the heart of the conspiracy. His name is all over the first part of the diary. He recruited Sanders."

"I read the diary too," Mallory said wearily. "I've told you as much as you need to know. Piece it together for yourself."

"All right, you've pointed the finger at Parsons. What about the others?"

"Ah God, Rainey, most of them are dead or not far from it. What does it matter after forty-two years? They had nothing to do with any murders then or now. The man who just died in California sent Paterson out here."

"Can't you talk straight, for Christ's sake? If Parsons hired Paterson, why not say so?"

Mallory took a deep breath, then released it very slowly. "All right. All right. Here it is. You know so much, you might as well know all of it. But first let me tell you something. You should have checked on Mrs. Sanders before going to work for her. Mrs. Sanders was a bit cracked and it got worse as she got older—it usually does. As soon as Ritter got word to her about the diary, she began to indulge in all sorts of fantasies, or so I'm told. Apparently revenge was one fantasy, getting very rich was another. Revenge for her husband's self-wrecked career. Getting rich by blackmailing those named in the diary. You never caught on that she was nutty?"

"Eccentric yes, nutty, no."

Mallory was enjoying his put-down. "You should have caught on, Rainey. A wiseguy like you. Okay, Mrs. Sanders knew Ritter had the diary down there in the wilds of Mindanao. Ritter had it, but she thought it was just a matter of time before she had it. So she talked about what she was going to do with it. At night, usually, late at night, she drank too much and got on the phone to the weirdest people. Like Martha Mitchell, she couldn't shut up. People told other people. The news spread. You got here too late, Rainey—not that it would have made any difference. They'd have tortured and killed her anyway."

"Who was Paterson?"

"Head of the Parsons company private police. His real name was Frederick Bogardus. I don't know where he found the heavies, but he'd know where to find heavies."

"How did you get onto all this?"

"I just told you. Mrs. Sanders drank and talked. Word came to us in a roundabout way. You were on your way to Manila and that crazy old woman was still putting *your* head and *her* head in a noose. You still mean to say you didn't notice anything unusual about her?"

"She looked like she drank. She was drinking a glass of wine when I got there. I mean, she wasn't swigging from the bottle. Plenty of old people like a belt. It makes it easier to be old."

Mallory's smile was all malice. "A philosopher as well as everything else. Next time out, you'd better take a closer look at your clients. Ah well, we live and learn. You should be glad you're not going home in a coffin." Mallory checked his watch. "Come on, it's time for your plane. I'll see you off."

"No need for that. I can find the airport."

"I'll see you off, or maybe you'll go back under arrest. And don't tell me that isn't legal. Whatever the U.S. Army does is legal at the time it happens. You were a soldier long enough to know that."

"I know it," I agreed.

We went down and out to the street where a car was waiting. The driver was an American. He looked at me with only faint interest.

Mallory didn't have to tell him where to go.

"That's a terrible life you lead," Mallory said while the driver was nudging his way through the bumper to bumper traffic to downtown Manila. "I think you'd be well advised to give it up."

"Enough about me," I said. "Now how about telling me the rest of it. You left out as much as you put in."

Mallory pressed a button that rolled up a sheet of glass between us and the driver. The driver took no notice. "I thought we were finished with all that. I just saved your ass and you're still asking questions."

"*You* didn't bring the diary back. *I* did. The Chinese Communists would have the diary if I hadn't got away from them. Think of the field day they'd have with something like that. You and your men were last in the field during the whole race."

Mallory glared at me and I knew his dislike of me was no pretense. "We got here, didn't we? What the hell do you want from me?"

"I want you to tell the truth. I broke my ass keeping that diary from falling into the wrong hands and you're still handing me a line of shit."

Mallory was annoyed but wearily interested. "Such as?" he said. "Now what are you griping about?"

"I'll tell you. You say the government sees no point in investigating the conspiracy at this late date?"

"That's right." Mallory's voice was careful.

"Because of General Parsons."

"Yes."

"Was he that important?"

"He was a highly respected general officer, a war hero. Add to that the fact that he was extremely old. Other factors have their own importance. Rainey, what Sanders worte in his diary wasn't the entire story. Prominent Americans and Filipinos were involved and the U.S. government doesn't want to dig any deeper into the matter."

"Meaning a cover-up?"

"Call it what you like, there's a good reason for it. Good God, man, it happened nearly half a century ago! What are you, the avenging angel? I'm sick and tired of talking about it. Spit it out! What the hell are you hinting at?"

We were out of the city at last. Overhead was the roar of jets landing and taking off. I'd be on my way home in about thirty minutes.

"I'm not sure what I'm getting at. Maybe what I mean is this. None of the people named in the diary are important enough to have caused all this fuss. What have you got? A handful of high-ranking officers, a few fairly obscure American politicians and businessmen, two or three middling famous Filipinos. A bunch of has-beens, really. There has to be more to it than that."

"Go on," Mallory said.

"Okay," I said. "A couple of places in his diary Sanders suspects that someone really big is masterminding the conspiracy. He never got to meet this mastermind, and he has no proof because of that. Just the same, he's fairly sure he exist. Sanders may have been a cantankerous old boy, but he was far from dumb. I happen to think he was right."

"Garbage! Where's the proof?"

"I just said there *is* no proof. I probably wouldn't have liked Sanders if I'd known him. No matter. Whatever he was, he wasn't a liar or a spinner of tall tales. There must have been a master planner. Don't forget that this was a secret plan to take over one of the richest countries in the world—underdeveloped but potentially one of the richest. A big scheme that called for a big man. A man who could unite the country under his leadership."

"Say the rest of it." Mallory's voice was cold.

"I think MacArthur was behind it," I said. "It fits. In the islands he was a little tin god and didn't want to give it up. The Japs wrecked his plan by attacking Pearl Harbor. He thought he could handle the Japs as he thought he could handle all lesser mortals."

Mallory stared out the window, tired and wanting to be rid of me. "You've got a sick mind, Rainey. If MacArthur is Mister Big, how come his name doesn't come up in the diary?"

"It *does* come up. Sanders came to MacArthur with inside information and he was told not to mention it again. I don't think Sanders was ever completely trusted and that's why he never learned about MacArthur. That fits too. MacArthur would only want to deal with those at the very top. The rich and powerful. Sanders was neither."

"Garbage," Mallory repeated, this time with less vehemence.

"No sir, I think it's the truth, the real reason for the cover-up. Truman may have fired Big Mac, but he's still a hero to the military. No one wants the great man's name dirtied up with an investigation of what really happened out here late in 1941."

The car pulled up in front of the terminal, but Mallory made no move to get out. "I want to say a few last things to you and you'd better listen," he said. "Drop this line of inquiry or the roof will fall in on you. We can make it very hard for you if we choose to. Are you listening?"

"I'm listening. How can I not listen?"

He gave me a sour smile. "What you've been saying, this throwing dirt on a dead man's reputation, well, none of it is true. But you better drop it just the same. It's dangerous and can only get you into trouble if you keep it up."

"I have no intention of keeping on about it."

"That's good to hear," Mallory said. "You shouldn't have brought it up in the first place. It's the biggest God-damned joke I ever heard in my life."

"Then why ain't you laughing?" I said, then got out of the car and hurried to catch my plane.